# MURDER BREAKS FREE

*Rooftop Garden Cozy Mysteries, Book 19*

## THEA CAMBERT

Summer Prescott Books Publishing

**Copyright 2022 Summer Prescott Books**

All Rights Reserved. No part of this publication nor any of the information herein may be quoted from, nor reproduced, in any form, including but not limited to: printing, scanning, photocopying, or any other printed, digital, or audio formats, without prior express written consent of the copyright holder.

\*\*This book is a work of fiction. Any similarities to persons, living or dead, places of business, or situations past or present, is completely unintentional.

CHAPTER 1

October had blown into the valley on a chilly breeze that was teasing the idea of becoming a wind. It had brought with it brilliant swaths of gold, red, and orange that draped themselves across the mountains, a transformation that Alice Maguire-Evans knew she would never get over. Every fall, without fail, it took her breath away.

Blue Valley, Tennessee—Alice's hometown—was set a little deeper into the mountains, a little further off the paths the tourists had beaten through the region. But that only made it all the more magical to the wanderers, the adventurers, who felt compelled to drive a little further, following the winding road around that next bend just to see where it led. Those folks were rewarded the moment they made that final turn to find themselves looking down into a valley, guarded on all sides by the ancient Appalachian subrange known as the Great Smoky Mountains.

The travelers who found their way to Blue Valley had no billboards to guide them into town. There were no brochures or roadside attractions like giant balls of yarn or life-sized dinosaur statues. Blue Valley, to the untrained eye, was a dot on a map—and a small one at that. But for those who did find it, it became a beloved place to return to, year after year. And at the beginning of October, it was the serious leaf peepers who were pulling into town, filling up the local campgrounds, inns, and hotels. The valley had been blessed by a cycle of warm, sunny days and crisp, chilly nights, plus a late first frost thanks to its ideal location, and, as Alice had learned back in high school biology, that was why the leaves were unusually brilliant in Blue Valley come autumn.

This particular Friday was of monumental importance to Alice, but it had nothing to do with the weather. This morning, she had faced one of the hardest challenges a new mother can go up against: dropping her baby off at Mom's and Dad's Morning Out for the first time.

"Was there a lot of crying?" Owen James, Alice's

best friend asked when she met him in Town Park after the drop-off.

"Yes," said Alice. "A *lot*."

"It was a tough morning," admitted Franny Brown-Maguire, Alice's other best friend and also her sister-in-law. Franny had faced the very same challenge that morning, but in her case, instead of a six-month old, she was dropping off her son, Theodore, who was just over two.

Owen sniffled. "The kids are growing up so fast!" Although he wasn't a blood relative, Owen was as close as family ever could be, and he and his husband, Michael, were both honorary uncles. Theodore's middle name was, in fact, *Owen*, and the beloved Uncle Owen was also godfather to both children. "I know Little Sprouts is nearby—"

"Yep. Right over there," Franny cut in, pointing directly across the street from where they were currently standing in the park.

Owen shot her a look. "And I *know* that it's the ultimate daycare center and that the kids will be well looked-after—"

"You've got that right," Franny interrupted again. "I don't think Theo's going to want to leave when we go back to pick them up in"—she looked at her watch—"three-and-a-half hours. He loves that place!"

"Wait a second," said Owen, looking back and forth between Franny and Alice. "I thought you said there was a lot of crying."

"Yeah, but it was all Alice and Ben!" said Franny. "The kids were doing just fine. Theo ran right off to play with the other toddlers, and Izzy was cooing up a storm for her teacher, Miss Cringle—showing off that little dimple in her left cheek."

Owen turned to Alice. "Are you kidding me? You *know* you have to put on a brave face for the littles! We've gone over and over this! You cried? What if Izzy or Theo saw you, and then decided Little Sprouts was a sad place, or worried something was wrong with you?"

"I couldn't help it!" whined Alice. "Suddenly, Izzy just looked so tiny and helpless. And what if she looks around and can't find me? What if she needs me and I'm not there?"

Owen shook his head. "Have you *met* your daughter?"

Isabelle Beatrice Evans had come into the world half a year ago, and was so spirited, independent, and smart that somehow, the nickname *Izzy* had stuck. Izzy's daddy—Alice's husband, Luke—was the valley's sole police detective—by all accounts, the strong, silent type—but even he had been moved by the dropping-off of their daughter that morning. Then again, he hadn't sobbed, like Alice and Ben.

Ben was Alice's brother, Franny's husband, and captain of the local police force. Franny and Alice had been best friends since their middle school days, and Alice had been tickled pink when her older brother had fallen for her dearest friend. But Ben and Alice, as that morning had reminded everyone, were criers. They cried at weddings, teared up during sappy movies and TV commercials, and practically wept openly every July, when they won the Independence Day weekend Pedal Boat Regatta. And *those* things were nothing to the heart-wrenching separation anxiety they'd endured this morning.

However, even Alice and Ben had to admit that it would be nice to have a few hours of their own here and there, not to mention for the kids to spend time in the company of other children. It helped that Little Sprouts was located where it was, in the heart of the historic downtown. Alice's bookstore, the Paper Owl, was literally a few steps away, as were Franny's coffee shop, Joe's, and Owen's bakery, Sourdough—all of which were housed in the same large building on Main Street. Ben and Luke, meanwhile, worked just around the corner, at the police station on Phlox. What was more, Alice and Ben's parents, Bea and

Martin Maguire, lived cattycorner from Little Sprouts, so they could sit on their front porch and wave or even join in when the children were brought over to the park for outdoor playtimes. Meanwhile, Franny's parents lived a mere block away on Azalea Street. So Izzy and Theo were pretty well surrounded by loved ones who could be at Little Sprouts within a couple of minutes, should they ever be needed, and this was the comforting thought Alice had clung to as she'd walked out the door at the daycare center that morning.

"We'd better get on with our run," said Owen, resetting the timer function on his watch.

The three friends had been preparing for the first annual Stuart's Notch Five-Mile Trail Run, which was set to take place the next morning. Owen had signed them all up on a whim about a month earlier as a way to help hold them all accountable as they got back to their regular exercise routine—which had been thrown off by Alice having a baby. And although their "runs" were approximately equal parts jogging, walking, and ambling along, they were definitely on the road to healthier lives. Still, five miles on trails was no joke. There would be twists and turns and changes in elevation to deal with, not to mention the occasional rocky soil. They set off for their jog around the park, which would then branch off into downtown and the tree-lined neighborhood streets around it.

"Nice and easy today," Owen reminded them all. "We have to save our energy. Something tells me we're going to need it tomorrow."

CHAPTER 2

The next morning dawned clear and cool. It was the absolute perfect day for hitting the trails at Stuart's Notch, which was probably why so many runners came out for the event. Far more than expected, in fact, which was why the park rangers were scrambling to register entrants and create alternate plans for channeling the extra runners through the park along trails that were too narrow for large groups.

"We'll have to create a few alternate routes," Alice heard Darcy, the head ranger telling Zack Spears, who had recently come to work at Stuart's Notch as her assistant.

Alice was thrilled that so many people had shown up that morning. It meant more money for the park, and that benefitted everyone.

While they waited for race time, the participants milled around in the clearing in front of the park's welcome center, everyone in great spirits, excited to be out on such a glorious day. Soon, the park rangers and the race volunteers seemed to have arrived at a plan for routing the runners, and Bobbie from Blue Valley Fitness, microphone in hand, announced that it was time for the warm-up.

Alice, Owen, and Franny attempted to follow along as Bobbie led the race participants in stretches, jogging-in-place, and leg swings, among other things.

"I hate these warm-up sessions," Owen grunted as they finished their final set of jumping jacks. "I'm not going to have any energy left for the actual race." He cinched the strap that held his fanny pack around his waist. "Fanny packs, clearly, are *not* designed to be worn during jumping jacks."

"What have you got in that thing, anyway?" asked Alice.

"Snacks. Lip balm. Bug spray. You know, necessities."

"Ugh," said Franny, bending to touch her toes like Bobbie, who was clearly one of those naturally flexible people. "If I pull a muscle before the starting gun even goes off, I'm taking Bobbie down."

"Look! There's the mayor. We're saved," said Alice, relieved to see Bobbie handing the microphone over to Mayor Abercrombie.

"Hello, and welcome to Stuart's Notch Mountain Park!" the mayor said. "I see lots of locals and lots of visitors out here today—which means we're raising a lot of money to help support our park and maintain these trails."

Everyone applauded. Owen nudged Alice and pointed to Ben and Luke, who were standing off to the side, both of them wearing baby backpacks with the kids tucked into them. Luke blew Alice a kiss and lightly bounced Izzy, who was very alert, looking quite pleased with her surroundings. Theo waved and clapped his little hands, then patted Ben on the head with exuberant force. Alice and Ben's parents, Bea and Martin, along with Franny's parents, Pippa and Albert, joined them and gave a wave.

"We have our own cheering section," said Franny, as she pulled her shiny brown hair up into a topknot.

Alice envied that hair. Her auburn curls, on the other hand, were already falling out of the rubber band that was attempting to hold them in place. She should've worn a hat.

"What is Mayor A talking about?" said Owen.

"I think he's giving instructions for the race," said Alice, who hadn't been paying as close attention as she should have.

"Who are all of these people in the hideous brown t-shirts?" asked Owen.

"Those are the race volunteers," said Franny. "See how the Stuart's Notch logo is on the breast pocket?"

"Plus the word *volunteer* is written across the back," added Alice with a smirk.

"Well, they should've picked an attractive color," said Owen. "Absolutely no one looks good in that shade of brown."

Alice had to admit he was right. She forced her attention back to the mayor, who was still talking.

" . . . that'll be the scarlet trail, to the north," he was saying. "And then you have your bright orange trail, your burgundy, your burnt orange, and your umber trails. Remember, everyone starts on the red and finishes on the gold. You've been divided into small groups so that the trails won't get congested, but that only affects the order in which you run the trails. By the time all is said and done, everyone will have gone five miles. So, be sure to stick with your group and stay on your assigned trails."

"What is he talking about?" asked Franny. "Whose group are we in?"

"We're our own group," said Owen. "I signed us up together, remember? Everyone here registered in one group or another. Look—there's Dr. and Mrs. Howard. I bet they formed a group too."

Doc Howard had been the cornerstone of the medical community in Blue Valley for many years, and had probably delivered half the local population—including Alice herself, as well as both Izzy and Theo. Mrs. Howard was the longest-running English teacher at Blue Valley High, and by the time you graduated, you definitely would've been in at least one of her classes. She was a cornerstone of the school. Both Alice and Franny had vied to be her favorite student. Owen hadn't arrived in town until after he'd graduated from culinary school, but somehow, he'd still managed to usurp both of them with Mrs. Howard. In fact, he'd quickly become a favorite with Alice's parents too. He bird-watched and fished with her dad, Martin. He baked and swapped recipes with her mom, Bea. And he even took ballroom dancing lessons with her Granny.

"Hello all," said Doc, who was jogging in place. "Ready to run?"

Alice smiled, noticing for the first time that he and Mrs. Howard were wearing matching sweatbands around their wrists and heads. "Ready as we'll ever be."

Mrs. Howard took Owen's arm. "Did you get time to read that book I recommended on the art of baking in Victorian England?"

"Loved it," said Owen. "Come to the bakery this week and I'll treat you to one of my new Leaf-Peeper mini-cakes, and we can discuss."

"Be sure to take advantage of the water stops along the route," Mayor Abercrombie was saying. "And if you need anything, look for the race volunteers in the, uh—" He turned to his assistant, Jake Shannon. "What color are those shirts? Almond? Chestnut?"

"They are *ghastly*, and they are brown. Brown, brown, brown," Owen muttered, earning him a playful swat from Mrs. Howard.

"They're certainly trying their best to use all the different fall colors," she said.

Doc leaned closer. "I'll admit I'm not sure what *chicory* looks like."

"Everyone, make your way to the starting line, and remember, start on the red, and finish on the gold. Any questions?"

Alice looked at Owen and Franny as they joined the other runners. "Do we know where we're going?"

"I'm sure it's all marked," said Franny.

"Piece of cake," said Owen.

"Mm. Cake," said Franny.

"I only wish Michael could be here to see us speed across the finish line," said Owen.

Michael Boyd, Owen's husband, was a brilliant poet as well as head concierge at the Great Grandaddy Mountain Preserve and Resort Lodge, which lay not far from Stuart's Notch in the shadow of the locally beloved Great Grandaddy Mountain. He was away for the weekend in Gatlinburg, at a concierge convention, and had hated to miss the race.

"Don't worry. Ben's going to try to film our finish," said Franny, doing a side stretch and accidentally hitting the runner to her right in the head. "Oh. Sorry!"

Before they knew it, the starting gun fired, and everyone took off down the red trail. A few minutes later, that trail branched off into other trails, which branched into others, each of them marked with a small sign swatched with one color or another. Doc and Mrs. Howard trotted confidently off in one direction, waving and giving the thumbs-up.

"See you at the finish line!" called Doc.

"Good luck!" added Mrs. Howard.

Alice looked at a trail sign. "Is that burgundy or merlot?"

"I think that's burnt orange," said Owen with a snort. "*Really*, Alice."

They jogged off into the trees and Alice thanked her lucky stars that she wasn't running the race alone.

CHAPTER 3

"Water!" Owen gasped. "Need . . . *water*."

"Get a grip, Owen," said Franny. "I'm sure there's a water station around here somewhere. It's only been forty-five minutes since the race started, and I don't think it's possible that you're dehydrated at this point. You drank about a gallon of water right after the warm-up."

"Don't remind me," said Owen. "It's still sloshing around in my stomach. I'm going to have to make a pit stop before too much longer."

"So you couldn't be thirsty."

"Somehow, I am."

"Does anyone have any idea where we are?" Alice had been wondering for some time now.

"We're on this trail here," said Owen, pointing up and down their current path.

"I can see we're on this trail," said Alice. "But which trail is this?"

"No idea," said Owen.

"Well it *was* the sienna trail," said Franny. "But I haven't seen a marker in a very long time."

"Or a water station. Or a volunteer in an ugly brown shirt," added Owen.

"I think we made a wrong turn somewhere," said Alice. "Franny, you brought your phone, right?"

"Yep," said Franny, waving her phone. "But I don't know why I bothered. There's no signal out here."

"Darn. If only we had a trail map, we could at least take an educated guess as to where we are and find our way back to the welcome station."

"Trail map!" said Owen. "I have a trail map. Hold on." He dug through his fanny pack and proudly produced a folded map. "That'll teach you both to make fun of a person's fanny pack." He walked over to a large tree and spread the map against the trunk. "Now let's see . . ."

"Wow, this park is bigger than I thought," said Franny, studying the map.

Alice squinted at the names of some of the trails, which were written in tiny letters. "Owen, this is the trail map for Smoky Mountain National Park. Not Stuart's Notch."

"Oh. Right." Owen rummaged through his fanny pack some more, but then shook his head. "Brought the wrong map."

"You don't say," said Franny. "Hey, have you got any gum in there?"

"The logical thing to do is to turn back and go in the direction we came from," said Alice.

"Unless this is one of the loop trails," said Franny. "Who knows? It might be shorter if we go on this way."

"You make a good point," said Owen, triumphantly producing a stick of gum and handing it to Franny.

"Okay, then how about this," said Alice. "We go on a bit further, but if we don't see any signs that we're getting closer to civilization, *then* we turn back."

"Works for me," said Owen.

They walked along in silence for a time, then Owen said, "We should make plans for later, after we get home."

"Why?" asked Franny.

"Because it would give us something to look forward to. Make us feel better. And it would take my mind off of the fact that I'm parched. *And* in need of a pit stop."

Franny just rolled her eyes.

"Okay," said Alice. "When we get home, let's go straight up to the rooftop garden and relax."

"Yes!" said Owen. "But I'll stop in at Sourdough first. I'll grab us all a post-race treat."

"And I should check on Hazel at the bookstore," said Alice. "She's still getting the hang of the job." Hazel was Alice's new assistant at the Paper Owl, and so far, was proving to be very capable.

"I'll run into Joe's and get us our favorite drinks," said Franny. "Then we can go upstairs and relax for a while."

"Sounds like heaven," said Alice. "Coffee, baked goods, the garden, and my favorite chair."

The rooftop garden really was a particularly relaxing place. The historic building that housed the Paper Owl, Joe's, and Sourdough was topped by three small apartments, where Alice, Owen, and Franny, along with their spouses, pets, and kids, lived when they weren't at their houses on the banks of Blue Lake about a mile from Main Street.

Years ago when the then-single and pet-free Alice had first opened her bookstore and moved into the apartment above it, she'd walked through the French doors that led from her small living room out onto the flat, empty rooftop, and she'd had a vision. The large open space, which was hemmed in on three sides by the building's façade, and the fourth by the apartments, was like a blank canvas, and as Alice looked at it, she envisioned pots of flowers and herbs, vine-covered archways, small trees, and twinkling lights. When Franny opened Joe's and then Owen opened his bakery, they'd both moved into the corresponding upstairs apartments and had shared in Alice's vision. Through the years, the three had worked together to create a cozy retreat above Main Street, complete with shaded sitting areas, a fire ring for chilly nights, a café table, and comfortable Adirondack chairs. It was the place to share everything from morning coffee to evening glasses of wine, to watch the sun rise over the mountains and set in glory at the end of the day.

When other shop owners had seen the rooftop transformation taking place, many of them followed suit, and these days, there were numerous such havens dotting the tops of the buildings on Main Street. Newcomers were always pleasantly surprised when they looked up and saw green spaces and twinkling lights crowning so many of the beautiful old buildings. Restaurants like the Smiling Hound, the local favorite pub, had even added extra seating on their rooftop, so that diners could enjoy their food and the breathtaking views of the town and valley at the same time.

The three friends had been walking along, making plans to look forward to for a few minutes when they heard a noise over to the left of the trail, a short distance off. They all froze and listened.

"What was that?" asked Alice.

"A sign of human life, that's what it was!" said Owen, turning left and cupping a hand to his ear to listen. "Hello! Is anyone there?" he called.

The trees and bushes were thick, and the trail had so many tight turns that even though they could hear movement, they couldn't see anyone. They walked a little way in that direction, and soon heard the sound of running shoes pounding along one of the nearby trails.

"Oh, sweet humanity!" cried Owen. "We're going to live!"

"This way!" said Franny, taking the lead. "I definitely hear runners."

Alice saw a flash of brown through the trees. "A race volunteer! We're almost back on course! And I don't even care what trail we end up on. Let's just follow the other people until we get back to the welcome center."

"Yoo-hoo! You in the brown shirt!" Owen called, looking around. "Wait. Where did that volunteer go? *Why* did they have to pick a color that blends into nature so well?"

"I can see a water station through those trees," said Alice, picking up the pace and leading Owen and Franny away from the trail and through the tall grass. "Shortcut, right this way. Oof!" Alice found herself suddenly pitching forward and landing none too gracefully face down on the ground. "Ouch!"

"Alice what happ—oof!" Franny stumbled and landed right next to Alice. "What *is* that?"

"This is why we stay on the trails," said Owen, picking his way through the grass. "Plus I'm starting to itch. Do either of you know whether there's any poisonous stuff out here, like poison ivy or sumac or oak or whatever? What's that saying? *Leaves of three kill a fellow?*"

Alice sat up and dusted off her hands. "It's *red and yellow kill a fellow*."

"Well, thank goodness I don't see any red or yellow plants around here," said Owen, stopping to look around.

"No! I think that saying is about snakes." Alice looked back to see what had tripped her and Franny up. There was a mass of some kind hidden in the tall grass . . . a brown mass. "That brown is very familiar. It looks almost like . . ."

By this time, Owen had caught up and was looking down. He gasped and fell to his knees. "This is a race volunteer! Help me turn him over!" He felt for a pulse. "I think he might be dead!" Then he shrieked. "Oh, he's definitely dead!"

Alice scrambled to her feet and helped Franny up. "Are you sure?"

"Oh yeah," said Owen. "He's covered with blood!" He quickly stood up and hurried to stand next to Alice and Franny.

"Let's go get help."

But before they'd taken a step, there was a sudden movement a few yards away. Alice felt every little hair on the back of her neck stand up. Owen and Franny had seen it too if the way they were clinging to Alice's arms was any indication. Time seemed to stand still as they all watched a man—tall, with bright blue eyes—step slowly out from behind a large tree. In his hand was a knife, covered with blood.

"I didn't do it. I swear!" he said, a tremor of panic in his voice. "I didn't do it!" With that, he dropped the knife and bolted away in the other direction, disappearing through the trees.

CHAPTER 4

Alice's scream came out even louder as it was bolstered by Owen's shriek and Franny's cry for help, and it wasn't long before several race volunteers and curious runners rushed over, along with rangers Darcy and Zack.

"Looks like we have a volunteer down. This is the second fall we've had today. This is why people need to stay on the trails!" said Darcy glancing at the body. She started to kneel down, but her radio suddenly squawked. "Darcy, we've got a situation at the pond. It's an emergency! Get over here *now*!"

"On my way," said Darcy. She looked at Zack. "I'm leaving you in charge here. I'll be back as quickly as I can. You have your first aid kit. Use it."

"But—" Before Alice could stop her, she was gone. She turned to Zack, who was opening his kit and preparing to kneel down next to the body. "That's not going to be of any use, I'm afraid."

"But—"

"Run get Doc Howard."

Zack snapped the kit shut. "I think he and Mrs. Howard had just crossed the finish line before we came over here."

"Seriously? *Already*?" said Franny.

"Bring Luke and Ben too," Alice called behind Zack as he ran off.

Race participants were jogging past them, many casting inquiring glances their way. In an effort to avoid causing a panic, Alice, Owen, and Franny stood a little in front of the body and waved or nodded whenever someone frowned in their direction.

"Doc and the guys are all way over at the welcome center," said Owen. "It's going to be a long wait."

"The welcome center's right over there," said Franny, pointing over her shoulder.

Sure enough, the welcome center, which had been built in the style of a large cabin, was visible through the trees.

"We were *this* close to water? And a bathroom?" said Owen.

"We must've walked in one big circle," said Franny. "You can run over there now."

Owen paused. "I don't need to anymore."

Zack came rushing up with Ben, Luke, and Doc Howard in tow.

"One of the volunteers is injured?" Luke asked as they arrived.

"Or passed out, by the looks of him," said Zack.

Alice, seeing her husband, ran and hugged him tightly.

"Are you okay?" He drew back to get a look at her face.

"I'm fine." Alice felt the sudden urge to cry now that she was in his arms. "Where are the kids?"

"Izzy was ready for her nap and Theo was getting fussy, so your parents are taking them over to their house. They have that new playscape and your mother said they missed them yesterday since we felt compelled to take them to a daycare center." He smiled. "Franny's parents are going over too. They're all making an afternoon of it."

"So did this guy faint or what?" asked Ben, who had knelt down on the ground and was gently turning the body back over.

"He's not unconscious. He's dead," said Owen. "He was stabbed."

All eyes turned to him, and Luke rushed to the body, where Doc Howard was just feeling for a pulse.

"Yep. Appears to be a knife wound," said Doc. He looked at Owen. "How did you know?"

"Well for one thing, the knife is right over there," said Owen, pointing.

"We saw the killer too," said Alice. "A tall man. Blue shirt. Long brown hair."

"Which way did he go?" asked Ben, and when Alice pointed, he ran off through the trees in that direction.

Alice felt the same tightness in her chest she always felt when someone she loved was in danger. She looked at Franny, and Owen put arms around both of them.

"He'll be okay," he whispered. "He knows what he's doing."

Franny nodded silently and took a deep breath.

Doc Howard looked up at Luke. "You called for an ambulance?"

"They're on the way," said Luke. He turned to Zack. "Could you go watch for them and show them where we are?"

"Sure," said Zack.

By that time, Darcy came jogging back over. "How's he doing?"

"Not good. He's dead," said Luke. "Could you help us to block off this area?"

"Of course," said Darcy, who had gotten her first real glimpse at the body and had turned quite pale.

Within a few minutes, just as the ambulance siren could be heard arriving at the welcome center, Ben returned, out of breath and alone.

Franny rushed over and hugged him. "Thank goodness you're okay!"

"He got away. I'll call the station and get Dewey and Trimble out in the squad car. He can't have gotten far." He took out his cell phone and walked toward the welcome station where there was enough of a signal to make the call.

Zack rushed up with the paramedics and Doc waved them over. Meanwhile, Luke walked to the spot Owen had indicated and squatted down next to the knife in the grass. Alice, Franny, and Owen moved off a short distance to give Ben and Luke, as well as Doc and the paramedics, plenty of space to work.

Unfortunately, this was not the three friends' first

encounter with a dead body, and in fact, they had a history of helping the local police force to solve some of their most troublesome mysteries. It had gotten to the point where Ben and Luke, although they still begged the threesome to stay out of danger, had no illusions that they wouldn't butt in whenever and wherever possible.

"I need you three to give me a detailed description of the killer," said Ben, walking back over to them.

"I want to hear this too," said Luke, coming to join them, carrying the bloody knife in a plastic bag he'd gotten from the paramedics.

"I guess we can't technically be sure he *was* the killer . . ." said Alice, looking at Owen and Franny. "I mean, we didn't see him stab the man—and he did say he didn't do it."

Owen scoffed. "You'd believe a man hiding behind a tree and holding a blood-covered knife?"

"Hold on. Rewind," said Ben. "Tell us every detail from the very beginning."

Alice, Owen, and Franny told the whole story—of getting lost, of hearing the movement in the trees and seeing the swatch of what looked like a race volunteer's shirt (possibly the same shirt the dead man was wearing), of tripping over the body, and of the man in the blue shirt coming out from behind a tree.

"If he was the killer, why bother hanging around?" wondered Alice.

"You said he had brown hair?" asked Luke.

"That's right," said Alice.

"What shade of brown?" asked Ben.

"Medium," said Franny. "And it was longish—down to his shoulders."

"And he had a beard," said Owen. "Kind of scraggly. In need of a good trim."

Ben scribbled in the little notebook he always carried. "And his eyes—"

"They were striking. Bright blue," said Alice.

Luke looked at Ben and then closed his eyes and sighed. He turned back to Alice. "I want you three to go home, lock the doors, and stay there until you hear from us. Got it?"

"Okay . . ." said Alice. "What's going on?"

"You've just described Jax Titus to a tee."

Alice looked from him to her brother. "That name sounds familiar."

"Ten years ago, he was involved in a botched robbery that ended in murder," said Ben. "Filbert's Jewelry Store."

"That would've been right before I moved to Blue Valley," said Owen.

"I remember!" said Alice. "Mr. Filbert was shot."

"Wait. Are you saying the guy with the knife is the guy who killed Mr. Filbert?" asked Franny. "Shouldn't he be in jail?"

Luke nodded. "He was. Until two days ago. He escaped."

CHAPTER 5

Alice, Owen, and Franny wasted no time making the short drive back to Main Street. Alice called her parents and made arrangements to pick up the kids after they'd had a chance to check on things at their shops. Somehow, knowing a killer was out there somewhere on the loose made her want to have Izzy within easy reach. In the meantime, Martin assured her they would move the children's playtime inside and lock the doors.

"Don't worry, pumpkin. We won't let anything happen to our grandchildren. Promise."

"Thanks, Dad," said Alice as Owen pulled into the parking lot behind their building.

They went in through the back door, which opened into a long hallway that ran the length of the building. The hallway housed the beautiful old wooden staircase that led up to the apartments, along with doors into all three shops.

Alice carefully pushed open the door to go into the Paper Owl. She loved that her backdoor was a working bookshelf. In fact, most people who came and went from the shop never even knew it was there, and Alice rarely used it during business hours, since she was almost always in the shop before opening and after closing. Today, however, there were customers browsing the shelves—including the DIY section, which was the hidden-door shelf.

Alice popped her head around to find a very surprised customer standing there. "Sorry!" she said, slipping through the opening and closing the bookshelf behind her.

"Cool!" said the customer. "I've been coming here for years, and I had no idea that was there!"

"It'll be our secret," Alice whispered with a grin. She spotted Hazel, who was behind the counter ringing up another customer.

Once that customer left, Hazel brought Alice up to speed on the morning's business, assuring her that all was going smoothly. Alice quietly told her about what had happened at Stuart's Notch.

"Oh my gosh, should we close the shop?" Hazel asked, tucking a frizzy curl behind her ear.

"Ben and Luke don't think that'll be necessary," said Alice. "They suspect the killer is long gone. But do keep your eyes peeled for a tall man in a blue shirt with shoulder-length brown hair and bright blue eyes, just in case."

Alice went into Joe's to check on Franny, who was just telling Beth the very same thing.

"I knew a little bit about what was going on because Officer Dewey happened to be here ordering coffee when Ben called him," said Beth, her cheeks turning pink.

Alice, Owen, and Franny were all hoping the shy police officer would eventually get up the nerve to ask the equally shy barista out on a date, and had been providing gentle encouragement whenever possible. So far, the two had danced together at the Harvest Moon Festival, but they danced around their mutual affection almost every day when Dewey showed up at Joe's for coffee.

"I need to run upstairs before we go get the kids," said Franny. "How about a quick cup of coffee?"

"And a quick cookie," Owen said as he breezed into the coffee shop. "I brought a bag of my special autumn leaf iced cookies. We can take some to the grandparents too."

"Great," said Alice, whose stomach had just audibly growled. "The kids are safe and I'd love a minute to regroup and take a breath before we go over to Mom and Dad's."

"It's been one heck of a morning," said Owen, holding open the back door to Joe's.

They all trooped upstairs and into the garden. Alice had never felt more thankful for her favorite Adirondack chair. She sank down into it and chased a sweet bite of cookie down with a sip of hot coffee. A group of twittering birds was hopping around in the branches of one of the garden trees, a cool fall breeze was blowing by, and the morning was leading into a beautiful day—in spite of everything.

Franny turned her red ginkgo leaf cookie over in her hands. "Owen, these cookies are exquisite!"

Alice sighed contentedly and took another bite of her cookie—an orange oak leaf. "I'm sure Ben and Luke are right. The guy with the knife is long gone by now. The state police will catch him. I'm starting to feel better."

"Agreed," said Owen. "The last place that guy would want to be is here." He chuckled and took a bite of his cookie, a yellow maple leaf.

"I disagree."

The voice had come from the other side of the rooftop—the side nearest the door to Owen and Michael's apartment. They all turned to see the man —the very same man they'd seen at the park—sitting on the ground, leaning against the façade, petting Alice's dog, Finn. Her cat, Poppy, was curled up next to him, and Owen's dog, Franklin, was asleep at his feet.

"Would you look at our traitorous pets!" said Owen.

"You really should lock the backdoor to the building," the man said, offering a nervous smile. "Not to mention your apartment doors."

In unison, Alice, Owen, and Franny stood.

"Now look," said Owen, stepping in front of the other two and holding up his hands. "We don't want any trouble."

"Good. Neither do I."

"So how about if you just go, then?" said Owen. "It's, uh, that way." He pointed a trembling finger toward the door to his apartment.

"I can't do that. I need to talk to you."

"To us?" Alice couldn't help asking the question. Why would an escaped convict want to talk to *them*? Her heart pounded harder as she reached the logical conclusion. "Oh my gosh, you're here to kill us, aren't you? You know we saw you with the knife this morning, and you think we're witnesses or something."

"We didn't see anything! We promise!" said Owen. "If you leave now, we'll probably forget you were even here!" He waved toward the apartment door again.

The pets were roused by this commotion, but didn't seem at all worried.

"What kind of horrible guard dogs are you?" Owen grumbled.

The man held up his hands. "I know you already told the cops all about me. I'm not here to kill anyone."

"Then we'll just—" Owen took Alice and Franny's hands, and made a small move toward Alice's door, and in a split second, the man stood and whipped out a gun. The pets looked on, Franklin yawing lazily before nodding off again.

"I don't want to use this, see?" The man gestured toward their chairs. "Just sit down and hear me out. Nobody needs to get hurt."

They all did as he'd requested, and when Owen whimpered a little, the man looked at him. "Has anyone ever told you you look exactly like Knuckles

Vanderhooven? You know, the mob boss around these parts?"

"There's a *mob boss* around these parts?" asked Alice.

"An extremely *handsome* mob boss?" echoed Owen.

"Yep. Well, he's in these parts now. I heard he came from New York or something. That's what caught my eye the first time I saw your picture in the paper. The local criminals all know him. Lots of them have even worked with him. Everybody knows he takes people into the *family*, so to speak, on a pretty regular basis. He can make you or break you in that world. You know what I mean?"

"Not really," said Owen.

Alice jabbed him with her elbow. "Of course we understand."

The man nodded. "In fact, when I was reading the paper that time and saw your picture, another guy was sitting at the table next to me and he saw it too—and he was like, *what? Are you in cahoots with Vanderhooven? Can you introduce me when we get out of here?* And I was like, *no way, man! I'm just sitting here reading the paper.*" He chuckled. "The organized criminals around here are mostly into gambling and your more complicated burglaries. You know, that kind of thing. But anyway, that's what grabbed me the first time I read about you in the paper."

"The paper?" asked Owen.

"The *Blue Valley Post*. I have a subscription to it and read it in prison. You know, to keep track of what's going on back home."

"No, we don't know!" said Franny. "Let me get this straight. You saw Owen's picture in the paper and that's why you're here?"

"Not just him. All of you." The man looked around. "Listen, I don't have a lot of time. My name is Jax. Jax Titus. Yes, I'm the same Jax Titus who's been in the news these past two days for escaping from the state pen."

Alice cleared her throat. "We hadn't heard."

"I went to that race at Stuart's Notch this morning to talk to you because I read about you three in the paper. I'm a big fan. Like there was that time you nabbed that lady who killed that yoga instructor?" He chuckled and shook his head. "You three have got it going on! Anyway, when I escaped prison I came straight here to find you. I need you to take my case."

"Take your case?" asked Alice.

"I was framed. Understand? I didn't kill anyone."

"It doesn't look good that you were seen holding

that knife," said Owen. "And your fingerprints are all over it."

"I'm not talking about the murder today—although I guess I'm framed for that, too, now that you mention it. Oh man, they got me again!" He grunted and stomped his foot. "But I was talking about ten years ago, the murder I've been serving time for." He shook his head. "If I was going to stab somebody, I'd never use a Bladerunner29."

"What's that?" asked Franny.

"The knife you saw me holding. Heck, my pocketknife has better blades on it. Ever hear of the PocketPal2000?" He reached into his pocket and pulled out a chunky pocketknife, then put it back. "Knives are sort of a hobby with me. Knives, tools, hardware. I love all that stuff. Anyway, I've been sitting there in the state pen for years, reliving that day in my mind, and I finally figured it out. I know who killed Mr. Filbert, the jewelry store owner! Or at least I narrowed it down to a few suspects. So I watched and waited for my chance to escape, you know, so I could exonerate myself." He laughed. "I couldn't believe it when that ice cream truck came in and the guy left the doors wide open."

"Why didn't you go to the police or something?" asked Owen.

"I tried that. They won't listen to me. You three"—he pointed the gun at each of them—"you're not the cops, but you're even better. You solve mysteries. I need you to help me. Before they catch me."

"Don't you know that my husband is the chief of police?" asked Franny. "And Alice's husband is head detective?"

"Uh . . . no, I wasn't aware of that."

"Then you didn't read those newspaper articles very carefully, did you?" said Franny, crossing her arms.

"Franny," Owen said through clenched teeth, "let's be nice to the man with the gun."

"I skimmed a little, okay? You might find this hard to believe, but I didn't have a lot of time to read in the pen!" said Jax, waving the gun around. "Look, I've had *ten years* to think about this. And the way I figure it, the real killer had to be one of four—well, three—people. It was Bruno or Maxim or Darwin. It could've been this other guy too, but now I don't think so."

"Why?" asked Alice.

"Well, because he's dead. He's the, uh, the guy you tripped over earlier." He shook his head and pushed up his sleeves. "Man, I can't even tell you how amazed I was to see him this morning—and he was dead! That was a real shocker! That guy's name is Trey. I was just trying to find you three, and then there he was! You were *way* off course, by the way. I almost couldn't find you. You were nowhere near the burnt orange trail! I mean, what were you thinking?"

Owen sighed. "Don't rub it in, okay?"

"I guess Trey was a volunteer for the race," said Jax. "He was wearing one of those brown shirts. I always had a feeling that guy was okay. I guess he was turning over a new leaf or something."

"So let me see if I'm understanding you," said Alice. "The dead guy, Trey, was one of the guys who might've framed you for murder ten years ago—I mean, that's what you were thinking when you broke out of jail?"

Jax nodded.

"So you had serious motive to murder him then, out of revenge."

"Well . . . yes, I guess so. But see, I just found him like that. I pulled the knife *out* of his chest. He was already dead!"

Franny's phone buzzed, signaling a text message. She looked at it, then up at Jax. "My husband is on his way here right now. You'd better run."

CHAPTER 6

In a panic, Jax ran over to the façade and looked down over the street. Then he looked around desperately, as though trying to decide on his next move. Alice held her breath, hoping that it wouldn't occur to him to take a hostage from among them and bargain his way out of town. All she could think about was her little Izzy, and how she needed to stay alive to be there for her.

"Okay, this is what you're going to do," Jax finally said, moving toward the door to Alice's apartment and throwing it open. "You're going to sit in those chairs—and stay sitting—for the next ten minutes. No calls for help. No moving." He pointed the gun at them. "Understand?"

They all nodded rapidly and then watched in

amazement as Jax stuffed his gun into his belt and pulled his shirt down over it.

"I meant what I said before," he said, pausing at Alice's door. "I didn't kill anyone. I need you to help me. Please." With that, he turned and ran through the apartment and out the other door. They could hear him clomping down the stairs and then the backdoor opening and closing with a bang.

"Hopefully Ben will run into him down in town," said Alice as the three of them breathed a huge sigh of relief. "You'd better let him know Jax went out the back door so he'll know where to look."

"Actually, that text came from one of my coffee bean suppliers. I'm calling Ben now," said Franny.

"And that's how we do it," said Owen, clapping her on the back. "Good job, Franny!"

"If that guy was even slightly good at being a criminal, he would've taken our phones," she said.

They all stood and walked to the building's façade and looked down.

"And he also wouldn't run right down Main Street. There he goes!" said Alice, spotting Jax. "I can't believe it. He's headed in the direction of the police station!"

The Blue Valley police station was only a short

distance away, half a block down Main and then right on Phlox.

"Ben, he's going down Main, trying to blend in!" Franny barked into her phone. "He's walking in the direction of the station!"

Jax, who had come up the side alleyway from the back of the building and was still close enough to hear them as he attempted to casually stroll along the sidewalk, looked up, eyes wide. "Hey! I said ten minutes! Can't you tell time?" He stopped strolling and started running at top speed, dodging pedestrians, hanging a left on Phlox, and disappearing from view.

Franny updated Ben on his location, and Alice could hear her brother over the line, exclaiming, "*And lock the doors for crying out loud!*"

"We *did* lock them," Alice said loudly enough that her brother could hear. "*After* we came inside. He beat us here." She looked at Owen. "Could he have picked that lock?"

"I bet Hilda went out to the outside storage room and forgot to lock up," said Owen.

"Alice!" Ben yelled. "How long have I been after you to make sure that downstairs door stays locked at all times?"

"Okay," said Franny, holding the phone away from her ear. "You're going to have to call each other and yell at each other on your own phones some other time." With that, she ended the call.

They could already hear the sirens of the police cruiser heading down Phlox.

"There goes Dewey," said Owen, resuming his seat after checking the doors. "Hey, is anyone else feeling itchy?"

"A little," said Alice, scratching her ankle. "Let's talk about what's just happened here. Should we even consider entertaining the notion of helping Jax Titus?"

"What a name," said Owen. "*Jax Titus*. It's like his parents *wanted* him to grow up to be a thug."

"Or a superhero," said Franny.

"Regardless, it's abundantly clear that the man doesn't have very good criminal instincts," said Alice. "First, he gets caught holding the stolen goods *and* the smoking gun at a jewelry store robbery that escalates into murder. Then, he gets caught holding a bloody knife at the scene of a second murder. Just standing there! He actually drew attention to himself by telling us he *didn't* kill the guy."

"On the other hand, he did have a clear motive to do the deed," said Owen.

"The evidence is pretty damning," added Franny.

"Besides, how could we ever trust him? He just

held us all at gunpoint," said Owen, picking up his coffee, taking a sip, and setting it back down. "Darn. It's cold."

"You're right," said Alice. "I think just this once we should let the police handle it. I don't ever want to see Jax Titus again."

CHAPTER 7

In spite of everything—or perhaps *because* of everything that had transpired so far that day—the rest of the afternoon was relaxing and refreshing. Alice, Owen, and Franny, along with Finn and Franklin on their leashes, walked down to the Maguires' house, where they shared Owen's fall leaf cookies with everyone and then invited the grandparents to join them across the street at the Parkview Café for a late lunch. They sat outside, enjoying the fall weather and the delicious food, then crossed over to Town Park, where they strolled along the winding pathways and pushed Theo in one of the toddler swings for a while. Izzy even had her first ride in the toddler swing, with Alice holding onto her while gently swinging her, and this brought smiles and happy giggles. They played on the slides and bouncy butterflies as well, then said goodbye to the grandparents and walked back to their building, where they checked in with their employees and then went upstairs to put the kids down for their afternoon naps.

As it turned out, everyone took a nap, even the pets, and when Alice opened her eyes again, it was early evening and the events of the morning seemed miles away. It was almost as though she'd dreamed the whole business with the trail run and tripping over the body and then having the run-in with Jax Titus in the garden. If her ankles weren't itching so much, she almost could've believed none of it had ever happened. There must've been biting insects in that tall grass!

"Alice, get yourself ready," said Owen, popping his head into her living room door from the garden. "We're all going out to dinner at the Smiling Hound. Franny's getting Theo changed, and then we'll walk down and meet Ben and Luke at the police station."

Alice had come to love having Saturdays and Sundays mostly off from the shop, but unfortunately, Ben and Luke often had weekend duty—especially when there was a wanted criminal in the area. Hopefully by now, Jax had been captured. She found Izzy wide awake in her crib. She'd rolled over onto her tummy and was looking around, fuzzy head bobbing.

Alice reached into the crib and scooped her up, holding her close and dancing her around the room. "Let's go see Daddy," she sang. "Then we'll go visit Mr. Patrick and Miss Sophie at the Smiling Hound."

Patrick and Sophie Sullivan owned the pub, and were both big fans of little Isabelle as well as Theo. As Alice changed Izzy into her dress with the fall-colored stripes, she thought about how lucky she was to live in a town where everyone knew everybody else. Had Jax Titus grown up in Blue Valley? He was younger than Alice—probably would've started high school shortly after Alice and Franny had graduated. What wrong turns had he made that had led him to his current situation?

Alice slung her diaper bag over her shoulder and let Franny and Owen know she and Izzy were ready, and within a few minutes, they were all walking down the stairs, Owen carrying the lightweight pop-up strollers. Once outside, they tucked the kids into their strollers and walked down Main Street, looking into shop windows, enjoying the smells of fall, along with the scent of chocolate wafting out of Sugar Buzz, the local gourmet candy store. A little further down, and they could smell fresh, hot pizza as they passed Pie in the Sky. They crossed to the north side of Phlox and turned right, passing the community center, where auditions were being held for an upcoming mystery that was to be performed on Halloween weekend. When they arrived at the police station, it was almost five o'clock, and they were surprised to see Ben and Luke, who should've been wrapping up their workday, standing out on the front steps with a small group of people around them—mostly newspaper reporters and photographers by the looks of them. Among them, Alice spotted Jane Elkin, owner, editor, and reporter for the small local paper, the *Blue Valley Post*.

"Do you believe there's any danger to the local population?" Jane was asking, as Alice, Owen, and Franny found space to stand off to the side but near enough to hear.

"We do not," said Ben. "We're still looking, of course, but we think Mr. Titus is fairly far away by now, and the state police are searching for him as we speak. This criminal is elusive, to say the least, but we don't think he's in this vicinity anymore."

"So who was his victim today at Stuart's Notch?" asked a reporter from another paper.

"A man by the name of Trey Hilton," said Luke. "He had recently moved back to this area, and had been an acquaintance of Mr. Titus back when they both attended high school here in Blue Valley."

"The reason we're holding this press conference is because we need your help," said Ben. "Even though we believe Titus is moving further away from this area, he must be considered armed and dangerous. He is an escaped, convicted criminal with a history of violence. Please tell your readerships to be on the lookout and to practice utmost caution."

The press conference wound down with a few more quick questions, then Ben turned and went inside the station, and Luke came over to Alice and gave her a peck on the cheek.

"We just need to finish up one report. We'll be right out, okay?" He bent down to the stroller to pat Izzy's belly. "Then we can all go to dinner."

"Good. We'll wait out here."

Luke nodded and jogged up the steps and into the station, and Alice turned the stroller and made a beeline for Jane Elkin.

"I thought we weren't going to butt into this," said Owen, close on her heels.

"We're not," said Alice.

"Then why are you going over to talk to Jane?" asked Franny.

"Just out of curiosity. Nothing more," said Alice.

"Oh good," said Jane when she saw them. "I was just about to come over and ask you a few questions. I understand you tripped over the body at Stuart's Notch today?"

"That's right," said Alice.

She, along with Owen and Franny, went on to recount the story of their interactions with Jax Titus.

"That's amazing," said Jane. "I can't believe he held you at gunpoint! This guy has been an enigma since day one!"

"So you covered the story ten years ago, when Mr. Filbert was shot?" asked Alice.

"Sure did," said Jane. "That whole botched robbery still bugs me to this day."

"Why?" asked Owen, lifting Theo from his stroller.

"Because that robbery was so incredibly sloppy. I mean, think about it. Jax Titus kills a man—and he didn't even manage to steal a single thing. The police arrived and he was standing there holding the gun and the jewels. Like a deer caught in the headlights. It's nuts!"

"Was that Jax's only crime?" asked Alice.

"No, he had a record," said Jane. "He'd robbed Lucky's Quik Pik the year before. He was eighteen at the time—just barely old enough to be tried as an adult. He ran into Lucky's, held Willard Holcombe at gunpoint, and took the cash from the register—I think he got away with a few hundred bucks." Jane flipped her reporter's notebook closed and put it into her bag. "That gun was the same gun that shot and killed Mr. Filbert, and that happened just after Jax had gotten out on bail. So it was back to the slammer for him—this time, the state penitentiary. I can't believe he managed to escape. Frankly, I wouldn't have thought he was clever enough."

"We've only spent a few minutes in his presence, but I find it hard to believe too," said Owen.

"So Jax did both of those robberies alone, right?" asked Alice.

"According to his own testimony, he robbed Lucky's by himself," said Jane. "But he always claimed he wasn't alone at Filbert's. He said there were four other guys there." She dug through her bag and took her notebook back out. She flipped through the pages. "I had to refresh my memory, so I just reviewed the case. Here it is. He listed Bruno and Maxim Archer—they're brothers. The third was a guy named Darwin O'Shea, and then the fourth was the guy who was killed today at the trail run—Trey Hilton."

Alice looked at Owen and Franny. "Those are the same names he listed to us."

"But the others all had alibis," said Jane. "Apparently, they were together at Pie in the Sky, and they vouched for each other under oath."

"Well that seems fishy," said Owen.

"Mr. Filbert didn't have security cameras at the jewelry store? Or an alarm system?" asked Franny.

"He did have an alarm system, but he'd turned it off. See, Mr. Filbert was a bit of an insomniac. It's been surmised that he had a wakeful night, went down to the shop to do some paperwork, and was in the back when Jax Titus came in. So Mr. Filbert himself had disabled the alarm, and there weren't any security cameras because he'd never had any installed. Anyway, apparently Titus was in the process of robbing the place when Filbert came walking out from the back room and surprised him."

"So Jax shot him," said Alice.

"His name isn't even Jax Titus, you know," Jane said with a small smile. "It's Stanley Knickerbocker. He started going by Jax after high school."

"I can kind of see why he changed his name," admitted Owen. "I mean, *Stanley Knickerbocker*? Doesn't exactly jive with a life of crime."

"He just seems to have made one wrong choice

after another," said Jane, putting her notebook away and turning to go. "When they catch him, he'll be in prison for good. And there'll be no escape this time." With a little salute, she started off down the street toward the newspaper office.

"Hey Jane," Alice called behind her.

Jane turned back.

"Do you think Jax—I mean Stanley—killed anyone?"

Jane paused. "You know, I rarely say this, but I'm not sure."

Alice frowned as they watched Jane walk on down the street. "Maybe Stanley deserves our help."

"Alice . . ." Franny said doubtfully.

"We wouldn't be in any danger," Alice quickly added. "We'd just do a little research."

Owen sighed. "She's got that look in her eye, Franny. There's no point in arguing." He turned to Alice. "Where do we start?"

"At the beginning," said Alice. "At Lucky's Quik Pik."

CHAPTER 8

It was easy enough to come up with a good excuse to stop in at Lucky's that night after dinner. The weather was turning cooler, and Alice wanted to run over to the lake cabin to grab a sweater for Izzy—and Lucky's just happened to be on the way. Everyone in town knew that no one served a better chocolate-cream malt than Lucky's, and Alice insisted that she'd be happy to drop by and pick up enough for everyone. She'd correctly predicted that Luke, who'd been at work all day, would be craving some time with Izzy. He volunteered to cover bath time and Franny managed to work the same deal out with Ben. Soon, Owen was behind the wheel driving down Phlox Street in the direction of Blue Lake and Lucky's.

"Hopefully Willard will be able to remember what

happened when Jax—I mean Stanley—robbed Lucky's ten years ago," said Franny.

"I think his long-term memory is pretty sharp," said Alice. "It's more the short-term stuff he has problems with."

It was true that Willard Holcombe's memory wasn't what it used to be, and he had lately developed a tendency to wander about town, occasionally getting lost. There was a general understanding in the little town that if you saw Willard walking aimlessly about, you stopped and checked on him. He'd been managing Lucky's forever, and was perfectly capable of doing the job. Recently, his daughter Idella had come to Blue Valley to stay, moving in with her dad and buying the little convenience store, so they worked together at Lucky's and she was able to keep a close eye on Willard.

After a quick stop at Alice and Luke's cabin, where Alice ran inside and grabbed sweaters for both Izzy and herself, they went straight to Lucky's Quik Pik. Lucky's was very handy when they were staying out on the lake, which was at least half the time these days. It was so convenient to run in for diapers, milk, bread—or a slice of pizza or frosty milkshake—without having to drive all the way across town to Whitman's grocery store. Of course, the residents of

Blue Valley were unaccustomed to driving more than five minutes to get anywhere, since the town was so small.

The bells that hung above the door at Lucky's jingled as Alice, Owen, and Franny entered.

"Well hello, all," said Willard, who was standing behind the counter.

"Hi Willard," said Alice. "Hi Idella."

Idella was over in the refrigerator section, stocking pint-sized containers of ice cream. "Hey guys," she said with a smile. "What can we do for you this evening?"

"We're craving your chocolate-cream malts," said Franny, patting her stomach.

"I'd be glad to whip those up for you," said Willard, taking down a large Lucky's to-go cup. "How many do you need?"

"Five tonight," said Alice.

"Extra thick," added Owen.

"Michael still out of town at that convention?" asked Idella, coming over to help her dad.

"He gets home tomorrow evening," said Owen.

While Willard mixed chocolate ice cream, milk, and malted milk powder in a blender, Idella chopped up chocolate covered malted milk balls—one of the ingredients that made Lucky's malts extra delicious.

"Word's out all over town that you three came face to face with that Jax Titus guy who robbed this place," said Idella, not looking up from her work.

"Yep," said Alice. She glanced at Owen and Franny, then cleared her throat. "That's one of the reasons we're here. We were wondering about the details of that robbery ten years ago." She looked at Willard. "Willard, do you remember that?"

"Oh sure," said Willard, adding a dash of vanilla to the blender. "Fella came in here about this time of night. I didn't have any other customers at the moment, but he'd probably waited until the place was empty to come inside. He had me clean out the cash register." He chuckled. "Nice kid, as robbers go."

"Dad!" Idella stopped what she was doing and set down her knife. "He held you up at gunpoint! He was anything but a *nice kid*!"

Willard scoffed. "Pish!"

"And now he's escaped from prison! He could come back here!" said Idella, putting her hands on her hips.

"Aren't you scared?" Franny asked.

"Not one bit," said Willard. "The kid even apologized when he left. Took the cash, asked for a corn dog and a candy bar, and ran out of here. Never saw such a polite robber."

"Dad, you're not remembering—"

"My memory of the past is just fine, honey," Willard protested. "If you don't believe me, ask Doc Howard. He'll tell you it's just the recent stuff I get fuzzy on."

Without looking at a recipe, Willard added a touch of cocoa powder and a skosh of cream to the blender, then poured the concoction into cups. Idella added generous dollops of whipped cream and the malted milk balls, then put lids on the cups.

"For the drive home," Willard said, as he loaded all five into a cup carrier.

"Thank you," said Franny, taking the carrier.

"You know, they found out later that gun wasn't even loaded? The kid got out on bail pretty soon after that."

"Yeah, but then he killed Mr. Filbert," said Idella. "Dad, I think you got lucky that night. And I'll be very relieved when they find him and send him right back to jail."

"Killed Filbert? I doubt it," said Willard.

"Dad, he went to jail for murder!"

"That kid didn't seem the type. I even remember what he was wearing that night—a Blue Valley High School t-shirt. He just took a wrong turn in life somewhere, I imagine."

"And now he's escaped from prison and is somewhere out there," said Idella, waving a hand toward the door.

"I'm not worried," said Willard. He grinned at Alice. "What else can we get you kids?"

Alice smiled at being called a kid and dug into her purse for her wallet. "That'll be it for tonight."

"Hold on—one more thing," said Owen, plunking a tube of itch cream onto the counter.

"Oh good," said Franny. "I'm itchy too."

"So am I," said Alice, handing over the money.

They thanked Willard and Idella and drove back to Main Street.

"So he was wearing a Blue Valley High t-shirt," said Alice. "I don't know why I didn't think of it sooner. I know exactly who to question to pin down the character of this Stanley Knickerbocker."

"I was thinking the same thing," said Owen from the driver's seat. "There's one person in this town who's gotten to know every graduate of that high school for eons."

Franny leaned forward from the back seat. "Mrs. Howard!"

CHAPTER 9

"Perfect weather for a Sunday stroll," said Alice the next day as they all exited St. Helena's Episcopal Church after the morning service.

"Wish I could," said Luke. "Ben and I have to put in some time at the station to give the other officers a break. But we'll see you later."

"See you later," said Alice, giving Luke a kiss just as her parents walked out of the church.

"Alice, dear, how about if you all join us for lunch?" said Bea, bending closer to the stroller to pat Izzy's tummy. "I've already got a chicken roasting in the oven, so we have plenty." She spotted Franny's parents, who were just saying goodbye to Father Amos. "Pippa! Albert! Come over for lunch, why don't you?"

"Sounds great," said Pippa. "What can we bring?"

"I've got a chicken in the oven," said Bea. "How about a salad?"

"Great!"

"What can we bring, Mom?" Alice asked, stowing her diaper bag into the bottom of the stroller.

"Hmm . . . could you run by Whitman's and pick up some of those yeast rolls? I'll do potatoes when I get back to the house."

"Sounds perfect. I'm hungry already," said Alice. "I need to run into Whitman's anyway to stock up on diapers."

"I need a few things too," said Franny.

"Me too," said Owen. "Michael gets home tonight and we're all out of his favorite tea."

"You three go to the store. Let us take the kids," said Albert. "We'll all meet up at the Maguires'."

"That'd be great," said Alice, noticing that Doc and Mrs. Howard had just emerged from the church. "We'll see you in a little bit."

The grandparents took both strollers and walked down Main Street toward their houses, while Alice, Owen, and Franny waited for the Howards.

"That worked out nicely," said Owen. "Now we can find out what Mrs. H remembers about our friend Jax."

"Don't you just love fall? I can't wait to get out into my garden today," said Mrs. Howard when she saw them.

"Best time of the year," said Owen, offering his arm, which she took. They all began to walk in the direction of the Howards' house. "Did you plant turnips this year?"

Mrs. Howard nodded. "They're coming along nicely. They'll be perfectly sweet after a frost or two."

It was only a few minutes before they arrived at the Howard's house, which lay only half a block from St. Helena's, on the corner of Phlox and Azalea. The house was across the street from the hospital, and Doc's private practice was right next door, so no matter where he needed to be, his commute was extremely short. To the other side of their house was an old barn, and between the barn and the house was the Howards' pride and joy—their garden. It was an admirable endeavor, with rows and rows of fall vegetables and flowers currently growing there.

"Pick whatever you'll eat," said Doc, handing Owen a pair of clippers and Franny a straw basket. "The first frost is just around the corner, so the green beans and late-season tomatoes won't last much longer. The kale and collards will be fine even after the frost comes."

"And pick a few mums to take home, too," said Mrs. Howard. "They'll look beautiful on your dinner table."

"Hey, congratulations on your fast time at the trail run yesterday," said Alice, clipping a dusty lavender chrysanthemum.

"Thanks," said Doc. "It would've been a great morning if it hadn't ended in tragedy." He shook his head. "Have they caught the guy yet?"

"I'm not sure, to tell the truth," said Alice. "I know the authorities all over the area have been trying to locate him." She looked at Mrs. Howard. "The man they're looking for actually went to high school here. We were wondering if he'd happened to be in any of your English classes."

"I heard on the radio that his name is Jack or Jacks or something?" said Mrs. Howard.

"Jax Titus, but that's not his real name," said Alice.

"His real name is Stanley Knickerbocker," said Owen.

"Knickerbocker—oh yes!" said Mrs. Howard, a light dawning in her eyes. "I remember Stanley! Are you telling me that the killer on the loose is *him*? I didn't realize!"

"He was in jail for killing Gene Filbert," Doc reminded her.

"He escaped a few days ago," added Franny.

"Stanley Knickerbocker," muttered Mrs. Howard. "I just find it hard to reconcile the Stanley I remember with the image of a coldblooded killer."

"Really?" asked Owen, popping a tiny yellow pear tomato into his mouth. "So you don't think Stanley had the killer instinct?"

"Not a chance," said Mrs. Howard. "You know what? I just realized why the name Jax Titus rings a bell. Stanley Knickerbocker was an excellent writer—one of the brightest I've ever seen at that level. He used to write these thriller mysteries. He named his main character—the hero—Jax Titus." She chuckled, shaking her head. "No, Stanley was a good kid. But he had one big fatal flaw. He was too impressionable. He started trying to impress the wrong kids and that required him to make bad choices. I guess it was a slippery slope from small-time robbery to the bigger crimes. Such a waste!" She sighed. "No, I'd bet Stanley just got in over his head. And now he has to pay the price."

"Very sad," said Alice.

"If he hadn't fallen in with those Archer brothers," said Mrs. Howard, her voice tinged with regret.

Alice perked up. "The Archer brothers?"

"Mm-hmm. Bruno and Maxim. And then there was that no good Darwin O'Shea. And Trey Hilton—he was always getting into trouble."

"Now don't speak ill of the dead, dear," said Doc.

"I'm sorry, but it's the truth. Those boys were all bad seeds, plain and simple. I'll admit I held out hope for Trey and Stanley—neither of them seemed as bad to the bone as the others, if you know what I mean. They had good parents and lots of potential." Mrs. Howard sighed. "Stanley somehow glamorized the tough guys in his imagination. Probably saw one too many stick-'em-up movies." She snipped a baby squash and tucked it into Franny's basket. "I was none too happy to see those four at the race yesterday."

Alice froze. "You saw them at the race?" She felt her heart pounding the way it always did when they were about to have a breakthrough in a case. "*All* of them?"

"Yep," said Mrs. Howard. "Bruno and Maxim. Darwin. And Trey—that is, I saw him before his unfortunate"—she cleared her throat—"well, before his death. They all appeared to be race volunteers, which I must admit, surprised me. The only one of the gang I didn't see was Stanley—but of course, you saw him."

"Holding the murder weapon, right?" said Doc. "Did they find any fingerprints other than Stanley's on that knife, by any chance?"

"I happened to see the report on Ben's desk," said Franny.

"Happened to see it? A likely story," said Doc, raising his bushy brows.

Franny flushed. "Stanley's were the only prints on the knife."

Owen looked at Alice. "I guess it's possible that Stanley was telling the truth and that the killer wore gloves." He bent over and scratched at his ankles.

"Could be," said Doc. He frowned. "Owen, why do you keep scratching?"

Owen straightened up. "Because I itch."

"Let me have a look." Doc bent and lifted Owen's pantleg to reveal a bumpy red rash. "Poison ivy."

"Oh no," said Alice, who had been trying her darndest not to scratch all morning.

"I've got it too!" said Franny, scratching furiously at her arm.

"Stop scratching, all of you! Did you get off the trails much yesterday?" asked Doc. "There's poison ivy all over the place right now, you know. That's why Mayor Abercrombie told everyone not to get off course."

"Well as it turned out, we missed a lot of what the mayor was saying," said Owen.

"Ranger Darcy says they're going to be spraying it to get it under control, but they're supposed to wait until spring," said Mrs. Howard.

"Wait here while I run over to my office," Doc ordered. "I've got some ointment for you three."

"And I have a fresh batch of cookies I've been wanting you to try, Owen," said Mrs. Howard. "I'll be right back." She hurried off into the house.

"Call Ranger Darcy," said Alice. "Ask her about her list of volunteers from yesterday."

"Already on it," said Owen, who had taken out his phone. "Since it's Sunday, Darcy will be at the welcome center. They get some of their biggest crowds on—Oh! Hi Darcy. Owen here." He paused while Darcy said hello. "Listen, Darcy, we have a question about the volunteers at the race yesterday. You have a list of names, right?" He pressed the speakerphone button and then added, "Alice and Franny are here with me. We were wondering about a few of the volunteers."

"Hi Alice and Franny! Yes, I have the list right . . . hold on a sec . . ." Alice could hear Ranger Darcy rummaging through papers. "Here it is! What did you need to know?"

Alice stepped closer to the phone. "Were there any volunteers named Bruno or Maxim Archer?"

They waited while Darcy studied her list.

"Or how about Trey Hilton, or Darwin O'Shea?" asked Franny.

"Let's see . . . no . . . I don't see any of those names on my list. Wait—wasn't Trey Hilton the man who was killed?"

"Yep," said Owen. "And he was wearing one of the brown race volunteer shirts."

"He was? Oh that's right, he was! That's odd. He wasn't a volunteer. Why would he have one of our shirts?"

"We were wondering the same thing," said Franny.

"You listed four names, right?"

"Yes," said Alice.

"Well that explains it then!" said Darcy. "I was four shirts short yesterday! I was at a loss, because I'd double-checked the shirts against my list of volunteers in advance. Now I see what happened! The volunteers arrived early and checked in, then we sent them over to a table where they were supposed to pick up their shirts and nametags. But I had four volunteers—the last four to show up—come to me and say there were no shirts left. I thought that was strange, but assumed I must have miscalculated."

"You didn't," said Franny.

"Thanks for your help, Darcy," said Owen. "Oh, and for next year's run, be sure to consult with me about the race volunteer shirts, okay?"

"Okay . . . Why?"

"I'll explain later." Owen clicked off the call and put away his phone.

"So let's get this straight," said Franny. "The four guys—the very same four who Stanley claims framed him for the murder he's been serving time for—were all at the race yesterday. Why would they go there?"

"And then one of them ended up dead," said Owen.

"And there's Stanley, standing over the body, looking guilty as sin," said Alice.

"But Stanley told us the only reason he came to the race was because he was following us," said Franny. "He wanted to talk to us about clearing his name."

"I guess he could've run across Trey, remembered old times, and killed him in a vengeful rage," suggested Owen.

"With a big old knife he just *happened* to be

carrying with him?" said Alice. "That would point to premeditation—not an impulsive rage."

"And Stanley said he didn't even *like* that knife," said Franny.

Doc Howard came walking across the lawn from his office. "I'm giving you three tubes of this extra-strength cortisone cream," he said. "Apply it twice a day and call me if the poison ivy doesn't clear up within a week. Okay?"

"Thanks, Doc," said Alice.

"And next time you're out at Stuart's Notch, stay on the trails for gosh sakes!"

"Will do," said Owen.

Just then, Mrs. Howard returned with a paper bag filled with homemade cookies that smelled like cinnamon. Alice took a peek inside. Oatmeal studded with raisins and chocolate chips! Her stomach growled.

"I added extra cinnamon and just a touch of cardamom this time," said Mrs. Howard, tucking the bag into the basket with the vegetables and flowers. "You all enjoy them—and Owen, let me know if you like the recipe. It's an old one of Grandma Howard's and I'm still tweaking it."

"With pleasure," said Owen, giving her a salute. "We're about to go over to Alice's parents' house for lunch. These can be our dessert."

Mrs. Howard looked at the flowers in her garden. "I should take some of these over to Val Hilton."

"Hilton?" asked Alice. "Is she—"

"Trey's mother, yes. She must be heartbroken."

"So Trey's mother still lives here," said Alice. "I guess I don't really know the Hilton family."

"The father is long gone," said Mrs. Howard. "But Val lives over on Azalea Street just a few steps down from Whitman's grocery. That dark blue house with the white porch railing? Trey lived there too."

"He still lived with his mother?" asked Owen. "He must've been in his late twenties."

"He'd just recently moved back to town," said Mrs. Howard. "My understanding is that he'd moved away, but had been through a divorce not long ago. So he moved home and was living with Val while he looked for a job." She bent to clip a flower. "That poor woman."

CHAPTER 10

"Let's get some vanilla ice cream to go with the cookies while we're at Whitman's," said Franny as they approached the store.

"Great idea," said Owen.

"You know what else is a great idea?" said Alice, looking a bit further up the street and spotting the dark blue house Mrs. Howard had described. "Stopping by Mrs. Hilton's house to pay our condolences."

"Well . . . she does live right over there," said Owen. "We could just drop by for a minute."

"It would almost be impolite *not* to say hello," admitted Franny. "I mean, we did find her son yesterday."

A few minutes later, they were knocking on the door.

"Yes?" Val, who had frizzy blond hair held out of her face by a green scarf opened the door just enough to peek out at them.

"Mrs. Hilton?" asked Alice.

"Yes . . ."

"Sorry to disturb you, ma'am. I'm Alice. Alice Evans. This is Franny Maguire and Owen James. We—" She glanced at Owen and Franny. "Well, we were the ones who found your son Trey yesterday at Stuart's Notch."

"We wanted to tell you how sorry we are about what happened to him," added Franny.

Val opened the door wider, revealing that she was wearing a long purple skirt topped with a green belted tunic.

"I love your outfit," said Franny, who's style generally danced the line between boho chic and free-spirited comfort.

"Thanks," said Val, smiling. "Come in. Have a seat."

They all followed her into a comfortable living room and sat in a row on the couch, opposite Val.

"So you found Trey? Was he—" She paused and looked at her hands, which were tightly clasped in her lap. "I don't even know what I'm trying to ask."

Alice leaned forward a little. "Mrs. Hilton—"

"Please. Call me Val."

"Val, from what we saw, it was very clear that Trey would have died instantly. He wouldn't have suffered."

Val's shoulders relaxed a little. "That's what Doc said too. That makes me feel better somehow, as horrible as this is." She gazed out the window. "And Trey was just turning over a new leaf. Or trying to, at least. He'd just moved back here after ten years away. His wife left him recently—but actually, that was a good thing. They'd gotten married years ago when Trey was still, well, taking wrong turns in his life. But in the last year or so, he'd finally come around. He'd decided to be a better person, and his wife didn't like that one bit. So she ran off with another man." She huffed a little. "Trey was better off. He was just living here with me until he could get a job and a place of his own. I was so glad." She put her face into her hands and cried.

Alice got up and went to her, laying a hand on her back. "I'm so, so sorry."

Val looked up at her, teary eyed. "Me too." She said, patting Alice's hand. Then she stood. "Let me get you a drink. How about some sweet tea?"

"That sounds great," said Alice, feeling like they needed to stay with the woman a bit longer.

"Good. You stay here. I'll be right back." Val went off to the kitchen.

Alice sat back down between Owen and Franny. "So, Trey moved away ten years ago—right after Stanley took the rap for a murder he might not have committed and went to jail."

"Coincidence? I think not," said Owen, crossing his arms over his chest.

"And then Trey moves back to town and gets killed almost immediately," said Franny.

Val returned with a tray holding four glasses of iced tea. Everyone took a glass and drank.

"You know, something had been troubling him, though," said Val, setting down her glass. She shook her head sadly. "My poor boy. He told me he had to clear something up—that it might involve him having to go away again for a while, but that he needed to right a wrong to clear his conscience. He said he wanted me to know that no matter what anyone said, he never hurt anyone." She looked at them. "What do you make of that?"

They all sat in silence for a moment, considering this.

"Val," Alice finally said, "do you have any idea who would want to hurt your son?"

"Well, of course, they're saying it was Stanley

Knickerbocker, but that's nonsense. Stanley was always a good friend to Trey. That's why I didn't call the police when he stopped by."

Alice almost choked on a swallow of tea. "He stopped by? Stanley did?"

Val nodded. "He told me how sorry he was about Trey. He promised me he didn't hurt anyone—not Trey and not Mr. Filbert, either. And he said he'd try to visit again, but it was possible he'd be going back to prison soon."

"The police think Stanley's probably long gone by now," said Owen.

"Well, they're wrong about that," said Val. "He was just here."

"What? *Today* you mean?" asked Alice.

Val nodded. "Left about five minutes before you arrived."

"Do you have any idea where he was going?"

"He said he wanted to visit his parents around the corner before he went to try to talk to the police."

Alice looked at Owen and Franny, then back at Val. "Where do his parents live?"

"Oh they died years ago. They're in the cemetery."

CHAPTER 11

Alice grabbed the arms of both of her friends and halted them as they all walked through the entrance gate at the cemetery, a short stroll from Val Hilton's house. She quickly pulled them off to the side of the gravel path that wound its way through the property.

"There he is," she whispered, nodding toward Stanley, who could be seen sitting alone on a bench among some trees up ahead.

The Valley Creekside Cemetery was aptly named. Set in the valley alongside the babbling Settler's Creek on a peaceful plot of land, it lay just a hop, a skip, and a jump down Trillium Street past the local school campuses. The entrance was defined by two gorgeous stacked-stone columns with *Valley Creekside Cemetery* written in scrolling ironwork arcing overhead between them. There was a sense of peace about the place, and Alice was reminded of her grandfather's funeral, and how she'd been surprised by that. There was nothing scary or even spooky about this cemetery. It seemed like a restful place, and the only sounds at the moment were the gentle breeze rustling the leaves, the gurgling of the creek, and abundant birdsong.

"Hold on," whispered Alice. "Let's give him a few more minutes alone."

"Do keep in mind," Owen whispered back, "that he may very well make a run for it the second he sees us."

"We can't wait too long or approach him too suddenly," warned Franny.

They crept from tree to tree, doing their stealthy best to stay out of sight, finally coming to a stop behind a large oak just a few yards from where Stanley sat, his back to them. In front of him were various grave markers, some clearly very old, some newer, all of them engraved with the Knickerbocker name.

"I just want you both to know that I never hurt anyone," Stanley was saying, his voice quiet. "I'm being punished anyway, and it feels like my whole life is passing by and I'm just . . ." He took a deep breath. "I'm just stuck." He leaned forward, resting his elbows on his knees. "I made some stupid mistakes—I know that now. You tried to tell me, but I wouldn't listen." He put his face into his hands. "I'm sorry."

Suddenly, from the other end of the cemetery, three men came walking up. Stanley started when he heard them approaching and quickly stood to go, but the short, stocky man grabbed him by the arm.

"Hold up there, Knickerbocker. No need to rush off. We're just here to pay our respects."

The tall lanky one laughed. "And dance on a few of these graves. That okay with you Knickerbocker?"

Stanley straightened as though mustering his confidence. "Hello Bruno," he said to the stocky man. Then he turned to the lanky one and nodded. "Maxim."

"Hey, don't forget about me," said the third man, tall with pale skin and a shock of red hair.

Stanley nodded at him. "Hello, Darwin. How've you been?"

The stocky man, Bruno, pushed ahead of the others. "We've been great. How about you, Knickerbocker?"

"The three stooges," whispered Owen from behind the tree.

"I think I've seen those guys around town from time to time," said Franny.

"What are they doing here?" wondered Alice.

"Seems like they've come here expressly to bug Stanley," said Owen.

It was true. The three were getting right up in Stanley's face, teasing him, and occasionally shoving him lightly, almost as though they were trying to see how far they'd have to go to get a rise out of him.

"Should we make ourselves known?" whispered Alice.

"Absolutely not!" said Owen. "If they start to turn violent, we'll call your husbands. Meanwhile, we need to listen closely. After all, these are the three who Stanley thinks might've framed him for both murders he's gotten himself tangled up in. Maybe we'll hear a confession or something."

"Hey, Knickerbocker, why did you have to go and kill our friend Trey?" said Maxim, shoving Stanley's shoulder.

"Yeah, Knickerbocker," said Bruno. "That wasn't nice of you. Not nice at all!"

"You know I didn't kill Trey or anyone else!" said Stanley, turning red in the face.

"What about that jewelry store guy? You killed

him," said Darwin. "That's why you're *supposed* to be in jail."

Stanley turned to him. "When are you going to stop believing everything these losers tell you, Darwin? I didn't kill Mr. Filbert and I didn't steal any jewelry. You were in the getaway car, so you didn't see how it went down. They set me up!"

"Jewelry?" said Darwin. "Nobody stole any jewelry." He laughed. "Is *that* what you thought we were—" A sharp look and a jab from Bruno made him stop short of finishing the sentence.

"You know what I think you should do—you know, to clear your conscience after all the wrongs you've done?" said Bruno. When Stanley just looked at him, he said, "Go to the police. Just go ahead and confess. You know you're guilty."

"Yeah, *Stanley*," said Maxim. "Be a good little boy and go tell them you're sorry."

"They're going to catch you anyway," added Darwin.

From the far side of the cemetery, near the small, ivy-covered building that was used as a workshop and for storage, a lawnmower motor could be heard coming to life. Mr. Hanover, the cemetery caretaker, pushed the mower out and began walking up and down the grassy lawn. The three bullies watched him for a moment, then exchanged glances.

"We'd better be going. We've got a boat to catch," Bruno said. "We'll come visit you in the slammer sometime."

"Yeah, Knickerbocker," said Darwin. "You did the crime, and now you gotta do the time."

"Oh—and don't worry: we'll make an anonymous phone call to the police and let them know we saw you here," said Maxim with a snicker.

"We should call Luke and Ben," whispered Franny.

"But they haven't confessed to anything," said Owen. "And technically, it's not against the law to be jerks."

The bullies jogged off toward the creek, disappearing among the trees.

"Don't worry," Stanley grumbled, sitting back down on the bench. "I'm going to the station now, so it doesn't even matter if they call the police." He looked back at the graves of his parents. "I'm going right now."

When he stood and turned around, Alice, Owen, and Franny had stepped out from behind the tree.

"Please," said Alice, holding up her hands. "Don't run, Stanley."

He frowned. "You know my name."

"We like Stanley a lot better than Jax," Franny assured him.

Owen extended his hand for a handshake. "And we believe you now."

## CHAPTER 12

"So you'll help me?" For the first time, Stanley's tight expression relaxed and he smiled.

"We'll try," said Alice. "But we're going to have to bring the police into this."

Stanley bristled at the idea. "The second you tell them, they'll arrest me. And they'll never believe my story—it's not like I haven't tried to tell them before."

They all sat down on the bench together. Off in the distance, the lawnmower sputtered and died, and Mr. Hanover could be seen pushing it in a cloud of smoke back toward the storage building.

"Franny, could you text the grandparents? Tell them we're running late?" said Alice.

"Already on it," said Franny, who had taken out her phone.

Alice turned to Stanley. "Those guys came so close to confessing to their involvement just now."

"Close, but no cigar," said Owen. "But I'd be willing to bet that with a little push they might let something slip."

"We should try to trick them into incriminating themselves," said Franny. "We've done that in the past."

"*That's* why I came to y'all for help!" said Stanley, jumping up from the bench. "I knew you'd think of something." He paused. "How do we trick them?"

"As the bard would say, *that is the question*," said Owen.

Stanley pointed at Owen. "Shakespeare! I like that guy. I was always too afraid to admit it back in high school, of course. Didn't want to be a nerd."

"And we can see where that got you," said Owen.

Stanley frowned. "Yeah."

Franny put her phone back into her pocket. "I have an idea. What if Stanley went to those jerks and said he's found evidence that they were the ones who killed Mr. Filbert?"

"Then they'd kill *me*, wouldn't they?" said Stanley.

"I don't think so," said Alice. "You're their patsy.

They need you alive to take the fall for what they've done."

"Then again, they might kill you," Owen admitted. "It could really go either way."

Stanley swallowed. "Let's talk about this, guys."

Just then, Alice's phone rang. She took it out of her bag. "I bet it's Mom, calling to tell us to hurry up."

"I doubt it," said Franny, picking a small tomato out of the basket from the Howards' and popping it into her mouth. "I told them we ran over to the lake because Owen decided to bake a quick batch of cookies for dessert."

"Good thinking," said Owen. He reached into the basket and opened the paper bag of spicy oatmeal cookies. He gave them a sniff. "These smell amazing. Do you think Mrs. H will mind if we pass these off as our own?"

"Hey—it's Jane Elgin," said Alice. She answered the call. "Hi Jane."

"Hi Alice. Listen, I just found some very interesting information about Gene Filbert."

"Mr. Filbert? What is it?"

"He isn't dead."

"*What?*" Alice looked at the others. "Can I put you on speakerphone, Jane? Owen and Franny are here with me." She thought it wise not to mention Stanley's presence. Knowing Jane, she'd rush right over to get an exclusive for the paper.

"Sure."

Alice switched to speakerphone and turned the volume down enough that if Mr. Hannover should happen by, he wouldn't overhear the conversation. "You said Mr. Filbert isn't dead?"

Stanley's jaw dropped.

"Well, technically, physically at least, he *is* dead," said Jane. "But financially, he's very much alive—and running up lots of debts at the moment."

"Shopping from the great beyond?" asked Owen.

"You know the year Mr. Filbert died? He got a very generous tax refund—*which he claimed a month after he was murdered*! Since then, he's taken out at least one loan and run up quite a bit of credit card debt. Last month, he bought a fishing boat!"

Stanley clapped a hand over his mouth, his eyes bulging. He hopped around like he almost couldn't contain his energy.

"So someone stole his identity!" said Alice. "Have you told Luke?"

"I'm headed over to the station right now. Have they caught Jax yet?"

Alice looked at Stanley. "Nope. Not yet."

"Let me know if you hear anything new. Gotta run!" Jane ended the call.

"So that's what they were up to!" said Stanley. He shook his head. "It all makes sense now! They kept talking about Mr. Filbert's status—you know, his financial status. They said he was rich as Roosevelt. I heard them talking about his credit limit and bank accounts. Stuff like that! They weren't after the jewels at his shop. They were after his identity!" He snapped his fingers. "I knew I saw Bruno stuff a bunch of papers into his jacket." He kicked a rock and it flew off in the other direction. "That was right before he handed me the bag of jewels. And my gun."

"So it was your gun that killed Mr. Filbert?" asked Alice.

"Yep. See, I did that convenience store robbery on a dare—Lucky's Quik Pik?"

"I bet I can guess who dared you," said Owen.

Stanley nodded. "You'd guess right." He looked at his feet. "I *still* feel guilty that I did that to Mr. Holcombe. But back in high school, the Archers and Trey and Darwin? They were the coolest. I couldn't believe it when they started hanging around with me. You might find this hard to believe, but I wasn't the smartest back then. Or very popular. And girls? Well, let's just say they didn't know I was alive. Anyway, the dares started out easy. Like when I bought this gun at one of those gun and knife shows—that's also where I picked up the PocketPal2000." He took the pocketknife out and fiddled with it. "I never even loaded that stupid gun. And I got caught after Lucky's—that's how bad a criminal I was. Caught my first time out! Anyway, I served my time, got out for good behavior, and who should be waiting for me but those guys—who I thought were my friends at the time." He turned around and sat back down on the bench between Owen and Alice. "I told Bruno I was done with the illegal stuff, that I never wanted to go to jail again."

"I bet that went over well," said Owen with a snort.

"That's the funny thing," said Stanley. "I figured he'd be mad or just tell me where to step off, you know? But Bruno was really nice about it. He said that kind of life wasn't for everyone and he understood, but asked if he could buy my gun." He held up his hands. "I know, I know. Sell a gun to a bad guy. Not a nice thing to do, right? But I was just out of prison, I had no money, my folks were mad at me"—he waved a hand toward the grave markers—"and Bruno insisted that he and the gang were also done with all that stuff—that he and his brother were moving out to their family's cabin and it was off in the middle of nowhere, and they felt they needed protection, just in case. They offered top dollar. I never wanted to see a gun again. So, I agreed to it." He put a hand to his forehead and rubbed it. "He told me he was going to be in town that evening, and to meet him outside Filbert's Jewelry Store." He held up his hands again. "I know, I know. That should've been a red flag or something. Live and learn. Anyway, I got there, he took the gun to look it over . . . Then suddenly, he turns and runs inside the shop."

"This was at night? Didn't you wonder why he was going into a closed jewelry store?" asked Owen.

"Yes, but he hadn't paid me yet—and no alarms were going off or anything. He'd just said, *hold on a sec. I'll be right back.* I thought something was wonky about the situation, so after a minute, I went inside the shop to tell Bruno the deal was off and I was going home. And next thing I know, he comes running from the back room with his brother right behind him, hands me a sack and the gun, and runs away. I was stunned. I went out onto the sidewalk and looked around, but those guys had driven off in Darwin's car. A few seconds later, the police drove up." He shook his head. "Bruno already knew that gun. He must've loaded it when he went inside."

"So the gun you held on us in the garden yesterday . . ."

"That wasn't even a real gun." Stanley sighed miserably. "I stole it one time when this theater group came through the pen and did a show with these gangsters in it. *Guys and Dolls*? And I'd managed to stash my PocketPal2000 outside the station that day the police took me in, when they looked the other way." He tossed the pocketknife into the air and caught it. "Like I told you, I've been planning my escape for a long time, working it out in my head. I thought if I could get out and prove I didn't commit murder, it'd be worth the risk."

"So the other guys had alibis?" asked Alice.

Stanley nodded. "And they, unlike me, had no criminal records. They, unlike me, weren't on record as owning any guns. And I don't know how he did it, but Bruno had even bought the ammunition in my name, so it looked like I bought the bullets just before the murder took place." He sighed. "Who would you believe?"

"It's been so long since it happened that any evidence of what really occurred no longer exists," said Franny. "We really need the Archers and Darwin to confess."

"We heard them say they had to catch a boat

before they left," said Alice. "What did they mean by that?"

"No idea," said Stanley.

Owen snapped his fingers. "Jane said they bought a boat recently!"

"That's right. A fishing boat," said Franny.

Stanley stood. "I know exactly where they are!" He started walking briskly toward the creek, in the same direction the others had gone. "That explains why they went this way when they ran off. They needed to cross Settler's Creek! If you follow the creek that way"—he pointed north—"it curves around and then widens before it empties into the river. The Archers have a piece of land in the bend there—the one I was telling you about, with the cabin on it. It's off by itself in the woods."

"Stanley!" Owen jogged breathlessly along beside him, trying to keep up. "Stanley, hold on! Stan—can I call you Stan? Let's stop and think about this before we take the plunge."

Stanley just kept walking until he came to a narrow place in the creek. "We have to cross here."

"Stan, we can't face them unarmed and without the police," Alice insisted. "We have to go for help."

"I'm not unarmed. I have my PocketPal2000! Look." He took out his knife and unfolded one of its many features. "This is the alarm whistle. When you're in trouble, first you blow this and it'll make them deaf and take them by surprise. Then"—he flipped out a pointy tool of some kind—"you bring out the gouger. You stick them with this, and you're—"

Suddenly, sirens could be heard coming from the direction of the cemetery parking lot.

"The cops! *Here*?" said Stanley. "Is no place sacred anymore?"

"Those guys must've really made that anonymous phone call," said Owen.

Within moments, the sound of running feet could be heard, getting closer fast. Owen grabbed Alice by the arm and pulled her along with Franny behind a tree. Stanley followed.

He sighed. "It's no use." He looked at each of them in turn. "I can't outrun them. Thank you. You were the first ones to believe me."

"Stanley, we're going to do our best to talk to the police," said Alice. "We'll tell them everything we saw. They'll help you."

"Thank you for thinking that. But without that confession, I don't stand a chance." He took Alice's hand and squeezed it, then stepped out from behind the tree, walking straight toward Officer Dewey, who had just run up. "I'm right here!" Stanley called, hands in the air. "I'm unarmed."

"He's not unarmed," whispered Owen. "He has his pocketknife."

"No he doesn't," said Alice, unfolding her hand to reveal the PocketPal2000. "He gave it to me."

CHAPTER 13

Knowing they couldn't keep the grandparents waiting any longer—and *not* knowing exactly what to do next—Alice, Owen, and Franny walked quickly down Trillium Street, made a quick stop at Whitman's for ice cream and a batch of yeast rolls fresh from the bakery, then walked on to the corner by the park, where the Maguires lived.

They all enjoyed lunch together and played with the kids, then went out to sit on the porch in the rocking chairs and visit. When both Izzy and Theo fell sound asleep, Bea told Alice and Franny to just let them stay—that she and Martin would bring them over as soon as they woke up.

Alice, Owen, and Franny walked back down Main Street toward their shops.

"Why do I feel so listless?" asked Alice.

"Because you just ate like five dinner rolls and you're having a carb crash?" suggested Owen.

"Or because you feel bad about Stanley," said Franny.

"You're right—well, you're both right if I'm honest," said Alice. "I keep imagining him there at the station, trying to tell this story that sounds . . ."

"Hard to believe?" said Owen.

Alice nodded.

"I checked with Ben," said Franny. "He said Stanley's in the cell, waiting to be taken back to the state prison. He said they'll do their best to look into his claims, but it doesn't look too good. And now Stanley has the added murder of Trey Hilton on his shoulders—although that's still under investigation."

"He's already got so many strikes against him," said Owen.

"Has either of you seen my phone?" Franny stopped walking and dug through her bag.

"Wasn't it in your pocket?" asked Alice.

"Yes," said Franny, patting her pockets and finding them empty. "But it's not anymore."

"I'll call Mom," said Alice, taking out her own phone. "Maybe it's at their house."

"It's not there." Franny slapped her forehead. "I

remember when we were jogging, trying to catch up with Stanley—I heard a little plop, like something falling on the ground, but didn't even think about it until now. I could kick myself for not stopping to see what it was!"

"It's a great day for a walk," said Owen. "And now no one can say we didn't get our steps in today. Let's go."

He pivoted and they all walked to Trillium Street, past Whitman's and the schools, and back to the Valley Creekside Cemetery.

"I'm sure we'll find it," said Alice, leading the way to the Knickerbocker family plot. "We just need to retrace our steps and then call Franny's number."

"There's no point in calling my number," said Franny. "I had the ringer turned off during church this morning."

"Hey, look at these cool aviators," said Owen, picking up a pair of sunglasses that someone had left on the bench. He put them on. "How do I look?"

"Kind of cool, but kind of shifty," said Franny.

"I'll take it!" said Owen.

"You should give them to Mr. Hanover," said Alice. "He probably has a lost and found or something."

"At a cemetery?" Owen snickered. "I doubt it."

Alice rolled her eyes. "Let's find the phone so we can go home and I can finish my carb crash in peace."

"Stanley took us that way, toward the creek," said Owen. "Franny, where did you hear the plopping sound?"

"Up there, closer to the creek."

They all walked along, scanning the ground as they went, but there was no sign of the phone.

"Let's fan out," suggested Owen. "I mean, I don't remember exactly where our path was when we were following Stanley. And Franny's phone is tiny." He raised a brow at her.

"Hey! Just because your phone is *huge* doesn't mean you're a better person or anything!"

"No. I just have a better phone," Owen said smugly. He veered to the right, while Alice and Franny veered left.

"You know what? It might've bounced a little after it plopped," said Franny. "It could've even gone into these bushes. I remember because they're right here by the narrow place in the creek where Stanley said we should cross."

"Oh that's right!" said Alice. She dropped to her knees and crawled into the bushes.

"I bet it's in here somewhere," said Franny, following.

"Look! Is that it?" Alice crawled in a little deeper. "Franny, that phone bounced a long way. You must've been running at top speed!"

"Thank goodness!" Franny crawled a little further, and sure enough, there was her phone, a little dusty but none the worse for wear.

"Hey—what do you think you're doing here?" an angry voice said from behind them.

Alice's first impulse was to assume it was Mr. Hanover, wondering what two grown women were doing crawling around in the bushes in his cemetery. But as it turned out, the person wasn't Mr. Hanover—and he wasn't talking to her and Franny.

"I—I, uh—" Owen was stammering like crazy as he faced none other than Bruno and Maxim Archer, who must've ventured over from their cabin down the creek.

"Well? Who are—" Bruno paused and scrutinized Owen for a moment. "Hey. You look familiar . . ."

In their bushy hiding place, Franny grabbed Alice's arm and held it in a death grip. "What do we do?"

Alice started to move, but then stopped when Bruno suddenly jumped back from Owen and said, "You're Knuckles Vanderhooven! What are you doing here?"

"You're kidding," said Maxim. "Seriously? Are you kidding me? You're Knuckles Vanderhooven? The mob boss?"

Owen cleared his throat and glanced to the side—looking for Alice and Franny in his peripheral vision, no doubt. "Keep your voice down, kid. You want everyone to hear you?" He'd taken on a sort of Brooklyn accent—and a wise guy attitude—in no time flat.

Owen had grown up in the theater in New York and had multiple acting credits to his name. Alice would've applauded his performance if she could have.

"I can't believe you're here," said Bruno, who didn't seem nearly as tough as he had earlier when confronting Stanley. "We were just talking about you."

Owen took a step closer to him. "I don't like it when people talk about me."

"No!" Bruno waved his hands. "Not in a bad way! We were just hoping we could, uh—" He glanced desperately at his brother.

"Meet you," said Maxim. "We thought maybe we could join your, uh, your organization. Someday, you know," he quickly added.

Owen chuckled, turning his head to the side so

that Alice and Franny could see his profile. He was enjoying this! "So you want my protection, do you?"

"Yes! I mean—we want to be part of something . . . you know, bigger," said Bruno.

"Look," Maxim offered, "our place is right through the woods here, just up the creek. Our friend is waiting there. Could you come over and hang out a little while?"

Owen paused, glancing to the side again. "Fine. But I got other places to be today. You better make this quick."

CHAPTER 14

As Owen and the Archer brothers crossed the creek and walked off into the woods, Owen glanced back over his shoulder, peering over the rims of his sunglasses. Alice eased out of the bushes and gave him a small wave.

"Come on, before we lose them," said Franny, reaching up to pull out a small branch that was caught in Alice's hair.

"Ouch."

"Sorry."

They carefully stepped onto the stones they'd seen the others use to cross the water, then crept along at a safe distance behind them, following the contour of the creek until, just as Stanley had described it, they saw a sharp bend to the left. Sure enough, Alice could see the roof of a log cabin coming into view, and could smell a campfire burning. She and Franny edged closer, finding a large clump of brushy shrubbery just to one side of the cabin to dodge behind. Peeking out, they could see Owen and the others—the Archers coming to stand next to the campfire where Darwin sat, turning a homemade spit that was loaded with fish. Nearby, where Settler's Creek fed into the river, there was a small wooden dock with a very nice fishing boat tied up and bobbing in the water.

"Darwin, you'll never believe who we found," said Maxim.

"I don't care who you found. Did you find my sunglasses?" Darwin turned, and immediately looked apprehensive at the sight of the brothers returning with a third person. He took a close look at Owen, who just stood there, sunglasses firmly in place.

"No way," Darwin breathed. "That is not Knuckles—I mean"—he stood abruptly and wiped his hands off on his pants, then held one out to Owen. "Mr. Vanderhooven?" The young man was clearly as awestruck as the other two had been.

Owen, ever the actor, looked at the hand but didn't take it. "I told your friends here that I don't have a lot of time. I was looking for someone else—heard through the grapevine that the someone I wanted was seen hanging out in the cemetery."

"Well we've been there today. Maybe we saw this person," said Bruno. "Maybe we could help you out. Who were you looking for?"

"Guy named Jax Titus," said Owen. "Know him?"

"Brilliant!" whispered Alice, switching on the recorder function on her cellphone. "Go, Owen!"

Bruno looked surprised. "Yeah. We know Titus. What do you want with him?"

Owen slowly turned his head to look at Bruno. "None of your business."

Bruno looked abashed. "Sorry, Knuckles—should I call you Knuckles?"

Owen paused, then gave a small nod. "You know where I can find Titus? I'm looking to bring him into the family, if you catch my drift."

"*Titus?*" Bruno scoffed and looked at his minions, who laughed and shook their heads on cue.

"Look." Owen took a threatening step closer to Bruno. "Do you know where I can find him or not?"

"By now he's in jail," Maxim admitted.

Owen nodded. "That's not a problem. I've got people there too. Where's he at? The state pen?"

"Not yet. He's here in the local jail right now."

A slow smile spread across Owen's face. "Local cell's easy. I heard that kid managed to escape from maximum security, *and* he's got a solid history. Did a couple of hits. A couple of robberies. I definitely got a place in the outfit for someone like that. Yeah, he's gonna be a made man. A goodfella."

"He's watched one too many mobster movies," whispered Franny.

"He's laying it on too thick," agreed Alice.

But the thugs Owen was talking to didn't seem to question the ruse. They were eating up every word, turning green with envy that someone the likes of Stanley Knickerbocker was the chosen one and not them.

Bruno scoffed and shoved his hands into his pockets. "Man, there's something you should know about Jax Titus before you go making *him*."

Owen affected a disinterested, tough stance. If only he'd had a cigarette hanging out of the side of his mouth, the full affect would've been flawless. "What do you know about Titus?"

Bruno took a step closer, then glanced around. "Titus didn't do any of those things." He proudly folded his arms over his barrel chest. "We did."

Owen paused, looking from one of them to another. "You kidding me? Because if you're kidding me—"

Bruno shook his head. "Nope. We got off because Darwin over there used to work at the pizza place, and we were all *seen* there when the murder happened, if you catch my meaning. Airtight alibi."

"What about that guy yesterday? Didn't Titus stab him or something?"

"Trey Hilton?" Bruno glanced at the others and grinned. "He was threatening to make amends for the jewelry store. We couldn't let him do that." He chuckled. "Hilton thought we were going to that race to find Titus and *apologize*. Instead, we managed to shut Trey up and blame Titus for the whole thing in one go." When Owen gave him a doubtful look, he spread his arms wide. "It's true! Look around you, man. See that boat? We got that off old Mr. Filbert's credit. We got a good thing going here. We steal information—credit card numbers, social security numbers, bank account information . . ."

"Small time hijinks," said Owen. "Identity theft is old news."

"Not when you're stealing the identities of *dead* people," said Bruno. "It's very convenient that they aren't around to call the authorities, if you know what I mean."

"So Titus isn't into all this?"

All three shook their heads. "He's just serving the time for what we did," said Bruno. "I did those hits myself. Just didn't feel like going to prison for it."

"Yes!" whispered Alice. "We've got them now."

"I'm texting Ben," said Franny, shifting a little to take out her phone. She gasped. "What was that?"

"What was what?"

"Something just slithered up my leg—something long and—slithering—oh my gosh!" Franny stood and jumped around desperately. "*Snake!*" she screamed. She glanced at Alice, a look of utter desperation in her eyes, then leapt out of the bush and strutted straight over to Owen. "So. This is where you got off to, Knuckles!"

Alice had to hand it to Franny. She'd blown her cover, but had instantly taken on another. And she was managing pretty well to match Owen's accent.

It was a good thing Owen was wearing the dark sunglasses, because his eyes couldn't be seen, but his jaw dropped momentarily. He quickly recovered. "What? Are you *following* me?"

Bruno, Maxim, and Darwin were instantly defensive. And more than a little suspicious. Back in the bushes, Alice frantically texted Ben and Luke, but received no reply.

"Who's this?" Bruno asked.

"*This* is Polly McGee. My cousin," said Owen. He turned to Franny. "I told you to wait in the car."

Franny, who was turning red in the face answered, "Like I really want to sit around waiting for you!" She looked at Bruno and gave him a conspiratorial smile. "Boooring! Besides, I saw you going off with these guys. I wanted to meet them too."

"Polly, stop flirting with potential members, okay?"

"Ooh, are we taking them in?" Franny managed a giggle that sounded fairly authentic.

"I don't know about this, Bruno," Darwin said, taking out his phone and punching some buttons. "Is this some kind of trick?"

Bruno looked at him, then back at Owen and Franny. He looked closer. "That's definitely Knuckles Vanderhooven. I've seen his picture plenty of times."

"This guy?" Darwin said, holding up the phone, its screen displaying a photograph of the infamous mob boss.

"Yeah," said Bruno. "That's him."

"That's me," agreed Owen. "Not a great picture, but then, I didn't exactly pose for it."

Darwin scrolled a little further down the page. "Says here you're currently doing time in Riverbend."

"I—uh—" Owen stammered.

"And there have been no escapes from Riverbend for some time," Darwin continued, clicking off his phone. "Who are you, really? And are you wearing *my* sunglasses?"

"Listen, I am who I say I am. I don't care whether you believe me or not."

"Come on fellas," said Franny. "Let's all be friends."

Maxim glared at Bruno. "They know everything, thanks to your big mouth. Now we have to kill them too."

Bruno shook his head, stepped forward and ripped off Owen's sunglasses. "Hey, you do look familiar." His eyes moved to Franny. "So do you. Haven't I seen you two around town? Like, walking around in the park?" He handed the sunglasses to Darwin. "Darwin! Two pairs of cement shoes. *Now*!" He turned back to Owen and Franny. "Let's go for a little boat ride."

"A one-way ride," added Maxim.

A panicked look crossed Owen's face when Bruno took out a gun and held it on him. He took Owen by the arm and Maxim took Franny.

"You like to swim, *Polly*?" he jeered.

They started walking toward the fishing boat. Darwin was already there, loading some things inside. Alice looked around. She knew she would be powerless to help once her friends set foot on that boat. But what could she do? In a rush, she remembered the PocketPal2000. Without even thinking about the danger, she made her way forward, dodging behind bushes and trees until she was only a few yards away from the group about to climb into the boat. She was close enough to clearly hear Owen trying to reason with Bruno. Alice flipped out the gouger and the whistle and ran forward, blowing the whistle as hard as she could.

"What the?" Bruno spun around in surprise, letting go of Owen's arm to cover his ears.

Owen took the opportunity to shove Bruno into the water, and in all of his flapping around, Bruno dropped his gun. "I can't swim!" he yelped, sputtering and coughing.

That commotion was enough of a distraction that Alice was able to jab Darwin with the gouger, hard in his right upper thigh. "Who the—ouch!" He bent over in pain, grabbing his thigh, which was bleeding.

"Sorry," said Alice. "Maybe you'd better wash that off." She pushed him into the water as well.

Then Franny, taking advantage of the ensuing

confusion, did the same to Maxim. "Go help your brother!" she called after him.

They'd been so distracted, they hadn't heard the sound of the sirens arriving back at the cemetery. Nor had they noticed Ben and Luke running up, Stanley leading the way.

CHAPTER 15

It was evening by the time Alice, Owen, and Franny made it over to the Maguires' house to pick up Theo and Izzy. Bea made it clear that it was hard enough being the mother of a police chief and mother-in-law of a police detective without everyone else she loved deciding to hunt down clues and go after criminals. A group hug followed, along with the assurance that they would all be careful and try to stay out of trouble in the future. Of course, Alice crossed her fingers when she made that vow.

She knew as well as she knew anything, that she, Owen, and Franny were good at detecting—that when they teamed up, they had a gift for getting to the bottom of things. But it was more than that. There was something indescribably satisfying about helping to serve justice. And, Alice realized, there were a million different ways to do so, whether you were actually solving mysteries or just raising good children.

When they returned to their apartments and stepped out into the cool of the evening, they were surprised—and thrilled—to find that Michael had returned from his concierge convention, and had made a quick stop at the Smiling Hound on his way back into town. Three large paper sacks sat on the café table, and the heavenly aroma of juicy burgers and crispy onion rings wafted through the air.

"You can see why I married this guy," said Owen, beaming.

"I can also see why he's so great at his job at the Lodge," said Franny. "Like every great concierge, he knows exactly what people want before they even know it themselves."

"Well, I might have mentioned I was having my Smiling Hound cheeseburger craving earlier when I called Michael from the station," Owen admitted.

"I'm just glad you're all safe," said Michael. "And don't go solving any more mysteries without me, okay?"

"Fair enough," said Owen, reaching into a bag and pulling out an onion ring.

"Ben and Luke should be here any minute," said Franny.

Owen peered into one of the bags. "Did you get that extra cheeseburger?"

"Yep," said Michael, grinning.

"Who's it for?" asked Alice.

"A very special guest," said Owen.

Just then, Ben and Luke came through the French doors, into the garden, bringing Stanley with them. A free and exonerated Stanley. The pets ran up to him, the two dogs wagging furiously, and Poppy purring and weaving around his legs.

"They always knew he was a good soul," said Alice with a laugh. "Hungry, Stanley?"

"Starving," said Stanley. He looked ten years younger than he had when they'd first met him standing there, holding that knife at Stuart's Notch.

They all found seats and enjoyed their feast, looking down over the Sunday evening bustle along Main Street—which was decidedly less as the weekend wound to a close. They all discussed the case, and how Alice's recording of the confessions of the Archer gang had been taken into evidence. The three men would be taking Stanley's place in prison and staying there for a long, long time.

"Do you resent the ten years you lost?" Alice

asked as she and Stanley played with Theo, who had gotten out the toy fishing set Alice's dad had given him.

Stanley chuckled. "Nah." He looked at her. "Nothing's wasted, you know. It all goes together and somehow comes out to be something good." He smiled. "Besides, I did a lot of good writing while I was in jail. Mrs. Howard has already agreed to look over my manuscripts and help me edit them."

"The adventures of Jax Titus?" Alice guessed with a grin.

"Yep," Stanley said proudly. "A man on a quest for justice and peace in this world."

"I'll want to stock them at the Paper Owl the minute they're published, okay?"

Stanley's smile broadened. "Okay."

Owen and Franny came over to join them.

"You're staying in Blue Valley, right?" asked Franny.

"Yep. I'm moving into my parents' old house." He glanced at his watch. "In fact, I've got to run. I have an informal job interview to get to."

Alice smiled. "Did Chester call you?"

"He did. And thanks for putting in a good word."

Alice's granny was married to Chester Lehman, who owned Blue Valley Hardware. Lately, he'd been telling Alice he was on the hunt for an assistant manager at the shop—someone who truly loved and understood hardware. Chester and Granny loved to travel and get involved in community life, so Chester needed help around the store. As Alice had waited at the police station to give her official statement that afternoon, she'd had the sudden inspiration to call Chester and tell him about Stanley Knickerbocker.

Stanley glanced down over Main Street one last time before turning to go. "I hope . . ." He paused and turned back. "I hope the town can accept me and forget what a stupid kid I used to be."

"Hey," said Owen, "you've already got a whole group of friends right here."

"Oh," said Alice, reaching into her pocket, "don't forget this." She held out the PocketPal2000. "And thanks for thinking to give it to me. It saved us today."

Stanley laughed. "It didn't save you, Alice. Your good mind and your courageous spirit—they saved you." He reached out and folded her fingers back over the pocketknife. "Keep it. I'll save up and get a new one." He gave another round of thanks to everyone, and with a little nod, headed through the door, into Alice and Luke's apartment, and down to Main Street.

"Now," said Luke, taking his wife's hand and

kissing it, "I'm going down to lock up. And then, we're all going to relax."

"I'll bring out a bottle of wine," said Franny, scooping up Theo and hurrying into her and Ben's apartment.

"I have a batch of my fall leaf cookies ready and waiting," said Owen, going into his and Michael's apartment, Franklin following at his heels.

"I'll build a fire in the fire ring," said Michael. "It's getting chilly out here."

A few minutes later, the kids were in their pajamas and the fire was crackling away, and everyone was seated and sipping wine while nibbling the delicious pastries. Alice could hear the crisp leaves chasing up and down Main Street on a breeze, their scent mingling with the woodsmoke and the wine. She closed her eyes and envisioned all of the blessings Autumn brought—walks in the woods, pumpkins and hot spiced cider, favorite sweaters and cozy movie nights.

"Halloween is just around the corner," said Owen, snapping Alice out of her thought bubble. "You know what we should do this year?"

"What?" asked Michael, poking at the fire.

"Throw an epic Halloween party."

After a beat of silence, Franny said, "I'm in."

Alice grinned. "Most definitely."

Owen sighed contentedly and leaned back in his chair. "Life is good, folks."

Alice took a sip of wine. She looked over at her husband, who held their sleeping daughter. She breathed deeply the new season that was just beginning and smiled. "It is indeed."

## AUTHOR'S NOTE

I'd love to hear your thoughts on my books, the storylines, and anything else that you'd like to comment on—reader feedback is very important to me. My contact information, along with some other helpful links, is listed on the next page. If you'd like to be on my list of "folks to contact" with updates, release and sales notifications, etc.… just shoot me an email and let me know. Thanks for reading!

Also…

… if you're looking for more great reads, Summer Prescott Books publishes several popular series by outstanding Cozy Mystery authors.

## CONTACT SUMMER PRESCOTT BOOKS PUBLISHING

Blog and Book Catalog: http://summerprescottbooks.com

Email: summer.prescott.cozies@gmail.com

And…be sure to check out the Summer Prescott Cozy Mysteries fan page and Summer Prescott Books Publishing Page on Facebook – let's be friends!

To sign up for our fun and exciting newsletter, which will give you opportunities to win prizes and swag, enter contests, and be the first to know about New Releases, click here: http://summerprescottbooks.com

Made in United States
Orlando, FL
21 September 2024